NO WAY OUT

By

Owen Seymour

A Patrick Spencer Mystery, Book 1.

For Ann, an unlimited amount of love and patience.

Chapter 1

He needed a coffee.

Fortunately, the first item unpacked last night on the clear, still, autumn Sunday and the most important to Patrick Spencer was his bean to cup Coffee Maker. Given as a present by Angelo Brioschi, close friend and owner of his favourite Italian Restaurant La Scala in Alderley Edge, Patrick rated this as one of the best presents he had ever been given and always used his favourite Brazilian Santos coffee beans, which gave a smooth earthiness to the finished brew.

His ideal morning always started with a fresh coffee, whilst listening to the honeyed voice of his long-term girlfriend Melanie Karlsonn presenting "A Good Read" on Radio 4, breakfasting on oven-fresh Croissants laden with his favourite Damson Jam and reading the morning's Daily Telegraph.

He and his partner Melanie had been a couple in most senses of the word, they were in love, slept together whenever the chance presented itself and enjoyed the same things, such as their love of horses, for over 4 years, yet they didn't want to move in together permanently. Both valued their independence and the opportunity to pursue their successful, individual careers was much easier living separately without the need to explain where they were or what they were doing on a daily basis.

The diminutive, five feet, one inch Melanie was Swedish, with curly, shoulder-length, strawberry blonde hair, striking sapphire blue eyes and a vibrant personality to compliment her archetypal Scandinavian looks and figure.

The daughter of Klaus Karlsonn, a commercial banker with Venture Capital company Diamond Resources plc in the City, she had received the best education available.
Attending Cheltenham Ladies College where she also benefitted from private music tuition from renowned former piano virtuoso Sir Peter Forbes, her father believed that the money was well spent as she was now an accomplished pianist in her own right although she seldom played nowadays due to her work commitments and the fact that she had no piano in her luxury third floor apartment in Manchester.

This was in stark contrast to Melanie's younger sister Melissa, a wild child who was expelled in her third year having been caught three times smoking marijuana and finally being in possession of a small quantity of cocaine. Only the determination of the College Principal to prevent a scandal and her father's generous contributions to the college (he had graciously funded a music scholarship) meant that there would be no police involvement.

The confidence gained from Melanie's education and her natural inbuilt resoluteness and determination had enabled her media career to progress rapidly and her current high-profile presenter role with the BBC was seen by many to be the first step to a glittering broadcasting career.

Her ability to speak 3 languages, English, Swedish and German, fluently with virtually no accent would afford her many more possibilities for progression and diversification. Her language was without accent that is until she became annoyed, which although not often, resulted in her native Swedish coming to the fore and her choice of vocabulary belying her education.

Monday morning, his first in the idyllic Oaktree Farm and dressed in faded denims and blue and grey checked Timberland shirt, he was barefooted and quickly decided that he had to do something about this as his feet were freezing on the cold Yorkshire stone kitchen floor, a kitchen in which he was still surrounded by numerous cardboard packing boxes.

He was acutely aware that even when everything was unpacked there would be plenty of empty rooms in his sprawling new farmhouse home which was a far cry from his compact bachelor flat above La Scala. He had therefore planned to start by furnishing the kitchen (in which to eat), the bedroom (in which to sleep), the lounge (to relax in) and the office (in which to work), the rest of the house would have to wait.

His decision to move to the peaceful village of Abbot's Meadow in the North Yorkshire Moors, just ten miles from his boyhood home of Malton, was to give himself peace and quiet to write the sequel to his first book and unexpected best seller.

Unexpected by Patrick that was, as having sent his manuscript to three publishers, he was shocked that two of them wanted to publish it and fought to tie him into contracts for this and any future books with the offer of what he thought were generous advances. The third publisher, Giles Armstrong-Hughes, a loud, rotund character, who was renowned for always wearing an old, frayed MCC Members tie, was however far more cautious and warned of the pitfalls of giving up his successful Police career (he was a respected Detective Inspector), the uncertainty of income (could he afford to give this up if the book didn't sell which it probably wouldn't) and the reality that most authors never see a penny of profit from their labours. This seemed to him to be a more realistic depiction of his future as a writer and he instantly felt that he could trust Giles, despite him having something of a questionable reputation.

Patrick usually made up his own mind about people, probably because of the experience of his occupation, and tended not to trust people until they proved him wrong, but with Giles he just had a good feeling.

Agreeing therefore that Armstrong Publishing would be Patrick's publisher, he would be fascinated to see if they could do what everyone else believed achievable, Giles thought improbable and what Patrick very much doubted, which was to make a profit from "A Time to Die".
Giles didn't however only publish the book but using all his experience guided it to number 3 on the Times Bestseller List, making Patrick a small fortune and an enthusiastic and eager fan base.

This enabled him to follow his growing passion for writing and leave his position with Greater Manchester Police after 22 years' service, mostly spent in the Metropolitan Police Serious Crime Squad, with a sizeable accrued pension as a safety blanket.

His parents had died in a pile-up in thick fog one Sunday, November night, on the M1 in Bedfordshire on their way back from a theatre break in the West End whilst the children Patrick and Amanda, stayed with their grandparents in York. It was thought best that Patrick and his twin sister Pamela, went to live with his mother's sister Penelope at their farm in Norfolk, leaving their childhood home in Malton. Despite the trauma of losing their parents, they both loved the farm and outdoor lifestyle.

He spoke to Pam occasionally but as she lived in Devon with her Farmer husband, Derek, they seldom met up. Only, like many elder siblings, at weddings and funerals and there was considerably more of the latter over the past few years.
Pam and Derek had never had children and never spoke about it, whether it was by choice or there was a problem he didn't know and had never asked, that was their business.
It wasn't that had fallen out, just that they both had their own lives, she had Derek and he had been busy building his career and the Serious Crime Squad also meant a serious number of hours.

He had visited them a few years ago for a couple of days after he had left the Met and before he joined Greater Manchester and they made him really welcome.

Derek showed him around their Dairy Farm, which, with a hundred and ninety-nine cows, was very impressive. The figure had always stuck with him as being illogical, why not buy one more and make the statistics easier to calculate. Still, it was not his farm. Despite having not seen his sister for five years before that, by the end of the second day, they had run out of things to talk about and he was secretly glad when it was time to leave.

Their parents, being from Yorkshire, had always been careful with money and they had left an estate, including two Prudential Life Insurance policies, of over £300,000 which was to be divided equally between the two children on their twenty-fifth birthdays.

Patrick had never needed to touch his inheritance so the gamble to change career was not as great as most of his friends imagined.

The twenty-two acre Oaktree Farm, situated on the outskirts of Abbot's Meadow and set adjacent to no less than three racing stables, was Patrick's first property purchase.

His previous jobs made it preferable to rent, so that when promotions occurred, he could move immediately and concentrate fully on the job, rather than on buying and selling properties.

The quiet of his new home after London and Manchester was almost tangible, and even though Alderley Edge was a wealthy and fashionable town, boasting many multi-millionaire footballers and businessmen cocooning themselves in large homes in small private estates, living directly above La Scala meant that there were hardly ever any quiet, relaxing periods.

The fact that Oaktree also had stables for six horses was a deciding factor, as both he and Melanie had a passion for horses and rode whenever they could. The countryside around the village meant that this would be an ideal retreat for Melanie whenever stayed, which was planned to be most weekends. She would soon be moving her horse, Torpedo together with Patrick's mare, Borea, from the stables in Cheshire to their new home and the quiet, leafy, country lanes and Patrick's sprawling land would be perfect for riding.

His first job, however, was to contact the Estate Agents to clear the stables of the previous owner's furniture. The previous owners had wanted a quick sale and, as Patrick had the cash to buy immediately he was able to save almost forty thousand pounds on the asking price.

The owners, however, had left hastily on completion, which suited Patrick's desire to start his new lifestyle, so when asked by the agent, he didn't object to them leaving "a few odd items" in the outbuildings for a short time.

However, the mass of furniture left was a concern and he would need the stables soon for their horses, so it was their horses, was it? Was he thinking about them as a couple again? He asked himself why this had happened a few times since he had agreed to purchase Oaktree, maybe there was a message there for him?

Looking around the cluttered kitchen he soon decided he needed a cleaner-cum-housekeeper. Having been used to having a housekeeper in Alderley Edge, the redoubtable Mrs. Poulton, who not only looked after his flat but left superb casseroles in the oven whenever he was working on a case, although he only had to walk downstairs for all the meals he could ever eat and for which Angelo refused to let him pay. After being spoilt like that, he didn't feel like looking after himself again full-time, especially as he expected to be absorbed in his writing.

Having spent such a short time negotiating with the agents and indeed viewing the farm only once, his only contact was the ever-helpful Julie at Oswald's Estates on the High St. in Malton and she promised him that they would arrange the removal of the furniture in the next few days. She also had details for the previous owner's cleaner, Audrey Weston, who lived in the village and had always been able to provide glowing references and Julie, therefore, agreed to ask Mrs. Weston to contact him directly if she was available and interested in taking on the position.

As it was such a beautiful morning, with the trees displaying myriad glowing red, russet, amber and gold leaves, Patrick decided to walk into the village to pick up a few groceries from the village store.
He always preferred to support local stores whenever possible instead of the big supermarkets, who he believed often failed to support their suppliers, and the decision to use the village shop which doubled as a Post Office was made easier for him as the nearest supermarket, Tesco, was some 10 miles away just outside Malton.
However, as he knew of no butchers' shop locally he thought that a trip to the supermarket would be called for some time soon.
Fortunately, he had a large, almost new chest freezer which he had bought to save the leftovers from Mrs. Poulton's "meals on wheels" so this shouldn't be too often, particularly living on his own.

He didn't concern himself with the Dark Grey, Land Rover Discovery with blacked out windows parked 200 metres away from the farm on his way into the village, assuming that it was watching racehorses from the neighbouring stables on the gallops, but with trained Police officer's instincts the vehicle had subconsciously registered with him.
However, on returning and having introduced himself to Michael and Annabelle Lampeter who owned the village store, imaginatively named "The Village Store and Post Office", the vehicle was no longer there.
He could however see someone moving in his kitchen.

Carefully turning the handle of the old stable-door style solid oak door, which opened directly into the kitchen, he quickly found the handle and hinges both needed oiling, he slowly opened it to hear the sounds of Ken Bruce's morning show on Radio 2 blaring out. Thinking it odd that any intruder would think to retune his radio from Radio 4, he tiptoed as quietly as he could into the bare brick-walled kitchen to find an attractive, ample-bosomed, middle-aged woman with short blonde hair, dressed in a pretty pale blue striped, shirt-collared blouse, slim fitting navy skirt which showed her shapely legs and wearing a pale blue and white gingham checked apron.

She was boiling the kettle on the AGA and writing what seemed to be a lengthy list, looking quite at home humming along to the Carpenter's "Yesterday Once More". So much at home that he noticed she was wearing a pair of well-worn sheepskin slippers, which spoiled her appearance somehow.

"Who are you?" he inquired in his deepest voice.
"Ooh you made me jump", she replied turning quickly to face him and seemed to visually appraise him before replying.
"I'm Audrey, Julie said you needed someone so I'm just making a list of things that you'll need, don't you even have a mop and bucket in the place? Cup of tea? It's nearly boiling".
"Well I would have preferred to meet with you first but how did you get in?"
"I kept a key just in case as a man on his own usually needs looking after", and they talk about male chauvinism he thought to himself.

"Well, Mrs. Weston", his police-style of addressing people just by surname may have seemed a little too formal but he didn't feel first names would be the correct way to address his housekeeper (he had never thought of calling Mrs. Poulton Edith, had he?) particularly as she was old enough to be his mother, well, possibly just.

"To start with we'll need to discuss wages, hours and the like".

"I do Mondays, Wednesday and Fridays from 9 o'clock 'til 12 same as before", interrupted Audrey "and you can pay me £6 an hour like everyone else, cash in hand. So, I've made a start. I'll buy the stuff you need and you can pay me, back shall I?"

It seemed that Patrick had found his housekeeper after what was undoubtedly the shortest interview ever but after all she did come with a recommendation from the agent.

"Tell me Mrs. Weston, who else has keys to the house?"

"I have keys to the house, all except the office, Mr. Novotny always kept that private, and Dennis, that's Mr. Marsh the gardener, I've had a word by the way and he's prepared to stay on if that's alright? he has keys to all the outbuildings except the stables. Mr. Novotny never let anyone go in there even though he had no horses, we always thought that was a bit funny".

The Office had been constructed in the roof of the original farmhouse which was built in 1826 and was all bare stone and red brick with exposed dark, weathered oak beams.

The natural daylight was from two newly installed Velux Skylite windows and the office floor was covered in a deep, luxurious bottle green Wilton carpet with a small diamond motif.

He must have left in a hurry Patrick thought to himself, as the office contained an antique mahogany, double-pedestal desk with an inlaid top in dark green fine leather with gold tooling and although Patrick didn't know a lot about antiques, he reckoned this must be worth the best part of £4000. The office door was solid dark oak but the biggest surprise was the high-security lock, designed to resist picking, kicking-in, and drilling. Patrick had knowledge of this type of lock when the Police were unable to break into a house in Hyde for two minutes, giving the occupants time to escape via a loft connection to three adjacent properties. But why the need for this type of security?

With his curiosity aroused he went to look more closely at the rest of the house and was surprised at one of the more recently added stables, the one containing the hoard of furniture, which was also protected with a hideous amount of high-security locks, CCTV and what seemed to be a separate high-tech alarm system. The agent had left instructions for all the alarms including codes and labeled all the keys, so it was quite easy to open the stable where he was faced with a collection of fairly ordinary furniture and rugs cluttering his stable. But again, he couldn't help wondering, why all the security?

Deciding the windows needed cleaning, and wondering if there was a local window cleaning service, he looked from his bedroom at the great views over the picturesque Derwent Valley across the meadows to the ruins of the 13th century St. Peter's Abbey, and pictured the Abbots walking in the once impressive building from where the village took its name.

He saw a movement away to his left and turned sharply to see the Land Rover he had seen earlier moving away. Who was this?

This time, there was no reason to assume it could be watching any racehorses as the string would be safely stabled after morning work at the three nearby racing stables.

That's another thing I must do, he said to himself as he mentally added to his to-do list; call and introduce myself to the neighbours.

"Mrs. Weston", called Patrick, "Do you know anyone with a dark grey Land Rover Discovery with blacked out windows around here?"

"No, but I've seen one hanging around ever since Mr. Novotny left, bit spooky actually".

"OK, if you see it again, can you let me know as soon as possible, oh and see if you can get the registration number for me would you please?"

"Why is there a problem?"

"No, just curious".

Just then his mobile phone rang, at least he could still get a signal here which was a blessing in such a rural area and particularly as the new landline would not be up and running for at least a week, typical BT service he thought.

"How's t'outback luv, caught any sheep rustlers yet?" said Melanie in her finest mocking Yorkshire accent, presumably picked up from watching episodes of Emmerdale on TV.

"Hello you, I listened to you this morning, is that Jonathan Jenkins really such a dick or did he think he had to try especially hard for you?"

Jonathan Jenkins was the author of a new history of the Cold War and the subject of the morning's radio interview with Melanie that he had listened to earlier.

"He really is a dick, far too full of his own importance, anyway how are you settling in?"

"I've employed a housekeeper, or I'll rephrase that, actually, she employed herself, she told me when she's working, what I'm paying her and she's just making a list of what I need, just like you're here really!"

"You won't need me to come over this weekend, then will you?"

"No that's OK, she's not working weekends so I'll need some washing and ironing doing".

"Cheeky sod, I have a good mind not to come".

"Seriously though it's so quiet, you'll love it and the stables are getting emptied next week so we can bring the horses in a couple of weeks, Dave says to let him know and he'll arrange the horsebox for a few quid as long as it's not needed for anything else".

"Great, so I'll see you Friday night, I'll be there about 7pm so have the wine open and the steak ready!

Jag älskar dig, älskling (I love you darling), see you soon".

Whilst she spoke English probably better than Patrick, who had a mix of Yorkshire and London accents, she knew that he loved the sexuality and mystery when she spoke her native language and always called him älskling rather than darling.

"Love you too", he whispered, "see you on Friday."

A sharp hearing Mrs. Weston smiled to herself in the kitchen and thought to herself, this is going to be a happy place. She had no idea who his girlfriend was but thought absent-mindedly that Oaktree was large enough to be a family home not just a house.

The village had a choice of two pubs, much quieter than Alderley Edge with its 30 odd pubs and 60 plus restaurants to choose from.

The Margrave, re-named after the famous St Leger winner of 1832 and trained locally in Malton by John Scott, was an "Olde Worlde" pub set next to the village green in the middle of the village, which it seemed to have been built up around.

With low, almost black beams, real log fires, stone flag floors and built around 1750 this was the "Local" for the stable lads and allegedly many a good tip was to be had here.

In contrast, The Red Lion was a modern red brick pub, newly refurbished, thick carpets, central heating, owned by one of the large brewery chains and serving typical bar meals; average quality and seemingly expensive for the area. This was the haunt of the self-styled middle-class residents who had moved in around the village and objected to the bawdy dialogue and banter that seemed to be the norm in The Margrave.

Both were just a ten-minute walk from Oaktree Farm and as Patrick had little by way of food for dinner and the chest freezer being empty, he decided to have a pint in The Margrave before sampling the menu at The Red Lion.

Being a Police Officer for 15 years, he enjoyed a pint with the team after work, particularly if they were celebrating a result, but had faithfully drunk lager as opposed to spirits when out, as he had seen too many careers go down the pan because of alcohol addiction which was not helped by the constant stresses of the job.

He was conscious from his previous visits to Yorkshire that the choice of real ale was almost a religion and The Margrave was no exception with no less than five different hand-pulled cask ales and a varied selection of brewery draught beers.

When in Rome he thought to himself and asked the attractive young barmaid Angela Castle, daughter of the landlord Peter, what she recommended.

"How are you settling in?" she asked, leaning forward to show ample cleavage with the top two buttons of a crisp white, cotton shirt undone and with lustrous, dark brown hair falling almost to the bar.

"Settling in?" replied Patrick trying to keep his eyes level with hers.

"Just moved into Oaktree Farm, haven't you?"

"How do you know that?"

"Not lived in a village before, have you? You'll get used to everyone knowing everything that goes on whether you want them to or not. Married?"

"No, but I do have a partner" Patrick replied with a chuckle.

"Pity, what about a pint of Black Sheep to start with, always popular" she replied without pausing for breath.

His pint was seductively hand pulled and had a thick, creamy head which looked very appealing and he was forced to admit it tasted every bit as good as it looked. I could soon get used to the beer even if the familiarity of the staff may take a little longer thought Patrick, as he took his drink into a corner seat by the Inglenook fireplace, with its crackling log fire as the early evening had turned a little chilly, as early October evenings were wont to do.

The bar was starting to fill as evening stables had finished and Patrick asked the group of lads at the bar,

"Does anyone know who drives a dark grey Discovery with blacked out windows?"

"No one in the village but there has been one around for the past 2 or 3 weeks", replied landlord Peter Castle taking an interest for the first time.

Oaktree Farm had been unoccupied for just three weeks before Patrick moved in, could this be a coincidence? His instincts told him not.

"If anyone sees it again would you let me know?" he requested, looking around the pub.

"Who's asking?" came a voice from near the door.

Patrick still found not being able to use the status of his DI rank strange, but before he could speak,

"Patrick Spencer, he's just moved into Oaktree Farm" Angela answered for him.

Chapter 2

Irishman Stuart Mullins, overweight, mid-fifties, with thinning red hair, a broadening waistline, and a lyrical Irish brogue, ran a successful fleet of Horse Transporters together with his wife of thirty years, the volatile and demanding Stella.

From their base off Mill Lane in Pickering, the modern Mercedes fleet, finished in stylish Burgundy metallic coachwork with a broad silver stripe, specialised in transporting racehorses, show jumpers and whatever else was needed, all over Europe and was a familiar sight therefore at Customs Posts at ports such as Holyhead, Felixstowe, Hull and Dover and at racecourses across the UK and Europe, but particularly England, France and Ireland.

Mullins and Stella had built up the business from scratch, starting with an old, battered Bedford CF which Stuart hand-painted in the same colours as today's modern fleet and had grown by offering a top-class service at reasonable rates.
They had contracts to transport horses for many of the yards around the North of England who didn't want the hassle or capital outlay of buying and running their own horseboxes. Far easier just to pick up a phone and let Mullin's team worry about getting their charges to the course in good condition and at the right time, leaving them free to concentrate on preparing the horses and saving a wage employing someone to drive the truck.

Mullins was the eldest of seven brought up in Ireland in a strict Catholic family, the only Commandment they chose to steadfastly ignore was number 8; "Thou shalt not steal".

As a boy, he struggled to come to terms with the contradiction of the enforced visits to Mass every Sunday whilst knowing the family was usually on the wrong side of the law, in fact by the age of 12 in the small town of Blackrock outside Dublin where he was born and raised, he knew every policeman based at the local Garda station by name, uniformed and CID, and they all knew him.

With his father, often "going away for a while", he had to make the best of every opportunity to earn money to support the family and through no fault of his own became used to living a life where he and the law were often strangers.

Though Mullins felt that this was his duty as a family member, he had to admit to feeling a great exhilaration when stepping outside of the law and getting away with it.

He met Stella Dooley at a disco in Sallynoggin to the south of Dublin one Friday evening when along with two friends, the fifteen-year-old Mullins wanted the thrill of drinking pints of Guinness like his father and uncles and knew that he would not be served in his local.

Looking for his pals who had disappeared to the Gents leaving Stuart to pay for the round, he saw Stella looking at him and the two couldn't keep their eyes off each other all night.

He was mesmerised by her long, wavy, raven hair and piercing steel grey eyes, to such an extent that had anyone asked him about her figure, he couldn't honestly have told them. Stuart had always been a brash daredevil who was phased by nothing, until then, and it took him an hour of looking across at Stella and seeing her return his look before he eventually plucked up the courage to ask if she wanted a drink.

Asking if he could walk her home at the end of the night she just laughed, taking his hand and guiding him outside and showing him the collection of Travellers Caravans on wasteland opposite the club. After kissing her goodnight and agreeing to meet again on Saturday night he walked the three miles' home in the cold drizzle with just one thought keeping him warm.

Mullins had made many acquaintances in the racing industry through his business but counted only a handful as friends, one being trainer Michael Adams who owned Monk's Lane Stables in Abbot's Meadow.

They soon found that they had one thing in common, demanding wives who were almost impossible to satisfy.

Mullins transported all of Adams' horses and frequently went to the races with Michael or with his Head Lad Seamus Collins, particularly the better meetings such as Newmarket, York, and Goodwood. Their knowledge of horses meant that Mullins seldom came home having not won a significant amount from Adams' tips.

Stella, however, was never pleased with his winnings even though he almost always treated her to new clothes, meals out, short breaks in the sun and once, having won over £15,000 at an afternoon meeting at the notoriously difficult Newmarket October meeting, over £8000 of it placing £250 on Mothers Ruin to win the Cesarewitch at 33/1 which it duly obliged by two lengths, buying her a beautiful three-year-old black Mercedes-Benz A Class 2.0 AMG Sport.

He was intrigued, when on a rare visit to Royal Ascot as a guest on Ladies Day, he was feeling a little out of his depth when, although properly attired in grey topper and morning suit, he found himself sharing a box with several of Adams' owners including a Lord and a Knight of the Realm. Being careful to mind his P's & Q's he wished he was in the silver ring with people he still considered his own class and much preferred a pint of Guinness to the champagne that was flowing, even if it was all free.

Later in the afternoon, as Lord Shadwell had taken his party to the paddock to view his prized three-year-old filly, Magic Moment, before it ran in the 3.40pm Ribblesdale Stakes where she was expected to start as a hot favourite, he had been approached by two affluent looking Eastern Europeans.

Both immaculately dressed, the taller of the two, grey-haired, with a trimmed beard and a good six feet in height, introducing himself as Rada Bilic, wore gold cufflinks and an ostentatious gold Rolex, whilst the shorter of two, he discovered later to be Talal Petrov, was a muscular, barrel-chested and black-haired Russian who was the more conservative of the two. They looked like a pair of wealthy owners and perfectly in keeping with the other guests in the suite of private boxes, sipping champagne and chatting to the countless exquisite girls and lavishly attired more mature women, several looking as though the Champagne was testing their resolve to see the day through.

Engaging Mullins in conversation about the prospects of Magic Moments, they seamlessly switched the conversation around to the many highly profitable opportunities available to someone who enjoyed almost unfettered access to racecourses around Europe, particularly if that someone had transport and was open to a variety of cargoes, strictly legal of course.

Having sown the seed, the two turned and engaged in conversation with their younger partners, stunningly turned out in what must have been exclusive designer couture, delicately sipping glasses of Louis Roederer Cristal Champagne, leaving Mullins in no doubt that he had been sought out but unsure just what he had been targeted for.

It was two weeks later that he took the phone call.

He had begun to wonder whether it would ever come, although he was convinced that he had read the signals correctly, but the invitation to meet in London at Michel Roux Junior's Two Michelin Star, Le Gavroche Restaurant on Upper Brook Street, just off Park Lane, left him in no doubt that he had read the situation correctly.

A strong south-westerly littered with heavy showers was blowing across Hyde Park as an apprehensive Mullins entered the restaurant that Friday lunchtime in early July. Apprehensive because he knew that there was a proposition to come and judging by the style of the men at Ascot it would be significant. Dining in a restaurant like Le Gavroche was a new experience and he again felt uncomfortable, just as he did at Ascot, his usual dining experiences extending only to familiar restaurants around his home such as the Taj Mahal Indian in Malton and the Golden Peacock Chinese in York. Maybe keeping him uncomfortable was part of their plan?

Warmly greeted with a pre-lunch gin and tonic and after small talk about the weather, the three were shown to the secluded corner table with green velvet studded, high-backed seating on two sides and a matching green velvet padded, mahogany carver chair, which was taken by Mullins, a silver Pelican identified the table, even that being a marked difference from the customary plastic table numbers in Yorkshire.

Not until he had enjoyed Calamars Sautés En Persillade et Risotto a L'Encre De Seche followed by La Piece De Boeuf Grillee Echalote et Sauce Au Vin Rouge did they enlighten the still hungry Mullins, portion control had never been on his agenda, about the opportunity for which he had been so blatantly targeted.

The need for secrecy when "the Family" offered an opportunity, whether he accepted the proposal or not, was stressed with more than a hint of menace. Mullins was in no doubt as to the consequences of betraying "Family" confidences and that the offer that was about to come was obviously in strict confidence.

Bilic proceeded to tell Mullins all about his transport business, the level of knowledge they possessed was very disconcerting, how did they know all this? Companies House could give them the financials but the number of trips, the names of the drivers, the trucks and even the names of the regular clients? They even suggested that Stella would be impressed by the new level of income he could produce. He was extremely concerned.
It was as if someone had laid out a dossier on your life, including things you thought were a closely guarded secret, to demonstrate that there was nothing you could hide from them. He was under no illusion that should he get into bed with these people, there would be no way out.

Confirming that Mullins understood the consequences of hearing the proposition and declining, Bilic detailed the tasks and rewards. The operation seemed to Mullins to be a low-risk operation and he was intoxicated by the potential for further involvement offered should he demonstrate his readiness to follow instructions without question and above all, maintain discretion "whatever happens". Mullins knew the consequences but with the potential payoff from this operation, he was hooked, in fact, he was already mentally calculating the income and planning what this would mean for him and the exhilaration when he told Stella.

"Whoa! Stella", he muttered to himself, "how am I to tell Stella? or should I keep it from her?" Stella already knew all the details of his past, so why should she object to this venture? After all, she would get to share the spoils, the villa in the sun, the new Mercedes every year, his mind was already racing.

"Good, I'm pleased that you have decided to join us" stated Bilic, reading his face and with a smile he reached across the table to shake hands. He added, losing the smile, "you will be employing one of our people to help with the operation. He'll be with you next week. He knows how we work and how to get things done, he will be most useful to you".

On his way back home from Kings Cross, travelling on the East Coast Mainline from Kings Cross and changing at York, Mullins plenty of time to reflect on the conversation and hoped he had not bitten off more than he could chew.

If they knew all about his business and had decided that he could handle the job, why did they need to send one of their crew to work with him?

He would obviously be there to keep an eye on his business and he was not sure that he was happy about that, it would be like having a spy in the camp. However, he reconciled this concern with the money, the lifestyle and potential early retirement to the sun. He would have to see how it went although he knew that he was committed and couldn't see any backtracking now or in the future being as simple as giving your notice.

The following Wednesday morning Stefan Bălan arrived carrying just a military style kit bag and casually dressed in faded denim jeans and a khaki coloured jacket over a simple white tee-shirt and well-worn trainers.

Looking every inch, a middleweight boxer, from the broken nose to the V-shaped body and muscular tattooed forearms and biceps, the black-haired, unshaven Bălan spoke surprisingly good English, albeit with an Eastern European accent, and they found later that he also spoke French, Rumanian and Russian, making him a versatile enforcer for his Rumanian employers.

Stella, who had been surprisingly easy to convince about the new venture when Mullins had painted a picture of easily gained wealth and all the trappings that this would bring, had prepared the self-contained flat above the horsebox garage for their new employee with a new duvet and bedding, new towels and even a new flat screen TV in the small lounge.

Bălan made himself useful around the premises, helping clean the trucks, check oil and water levels and tyre pressures which saved the drivers a job, as part of the drivers' daily responsibility was to complete the checks personally and sign the record of these in the vehicle logs which were kept locked in the office, noting any defects and if significant enough to affect safety, repair them before they were allowed to take the vehicles out.

In doing this, Bălan ingratiated himself with the team and soon learned importantly who was who, as he would need to source a willing accomplice to act as driver whilst he was looking after the "Family's" business on trips.

When the drivers had free days, they often drank in "The White Swan" on Mill Lane, overlooking Pickering Beck, the night before. It was written into their Employment Contracts that they were not allowed to drink the night before driving, and besides they were all responsible drivers, but when they could go out they usually had a session.

During one of these sessions, Bălan listened intently to the financial tales of woe of twenty-six-year-old Connor McLaughlin.

Flame red-haired, six-feet tall, lithe and ex-Army, Bălan thought that his training might come in handy plus he learned that he needed money to pay off his ex-wife and was already three months behind on the alimony payments. Mullins certainly did not believe in overpaying his staff believing they should be grateful to have a regular job at all.

Two weeks after Bălan had arrived at Mullins, a brand-new Mercedes Transporter arrived out of the blue. Out of the blue, that is to the staff, who had previously always known when a new or replacement truck was arriving and vied for the use of it as the drivers tended to use just one truck and therefore treated it is their own.

The new arrival could carry two horses and had all the modern refinements such as a double bunk sleeper cab, microwave, TV and DVD player.

A few jealous looks were exchanged when the keys were given to McLaughlin, whose current vehicle was only two years old, and the keys to this one given to the newest recruit who was currently driving an eight-year-old two-horse transporter, which had shown to be unreliable during the last six months.

Mullins was due to take a couple of jumpers down to Newton Abbot the following Wednesday for Jonathan Billings, a small trainer outside of Wetherby and Bălan had chosen McLaughlin as the man to accompany him on the "special" trips.

This trip, however, was not a "special" trip but a recruitment day.

The first task for Bălan was to ensure that McLaughlin was as keen to be part of the operations as Mullins.

Bălan was a good judge of character and given McLaughlin's needs, he felt sure he had chosen the right man.

Satisfied that McLaughlin's financial needs had taken priority over any reservations he may have had, they stopped for coffee and sandwiches at Tamworth Services on the A42 where Bălan showed him exactly why they had purchased the new truck.

Using the same specialist converter in Europe whose identity would remain secret, at the rear of the cab, concealed behind the bunks, was a virtually undetectable false back, being unfastened by four concealed clips and letting down to reveal a tiny self-contained compartment. The hidden compartment was capable of accommodating up to four people, with its own camping style chemical toilet, its own lighting system and insulated heavily enough as to render it almost soundproof.

McLaughlin showed little surprise as he immediately understood why Bălan was there and in no doubts as to what the compartment was designed to carry.

His only question to Bălan was "How much?"

"That depends on the cargo my friend, but trust me you will be well rewarded. You just need to do as you are told and keep quiet. Understand?"

"Yes" replied a sullen McLaughlin seeing that he had been given a way of repaying his debts and saving enough to start a new life somewhere soon, he only needed a few grand.

The rest of the journey down to Devon passed quietly, with McLaughlin deep in thought and Bălan hoping that he had not misjudged his driving partner.

Chapter 3

Following a call from Bilic, for their second operation together, Bălan informed Mullins that they had chosen a flat race at Nimes, just seventy-five miles from Marseille, on the first Sunday in October, the same day as the Prix de l'Arc de Triomphe.

They reckoned on this being the ideal time to load a valuable extra "cargo".
All attention, including that of the most experienced security officers who would be at scheduled to work at Longchamp that day would be on the cream of international thoroughbreds gathered for Europe's most prestigious horse race and they would be caught up in the electric, pent-up fervour of the big race.

Compared to the attention received by the Longchamp meeting, the afternoons flat racing meeting at Nimes would appear to be a neglected also ran, even though the prize money was considerably more than was on offer at English tracks that day.

On a bright, sunny but unseasonably cool August morning a conspiratorial Mullins, whilst accepting Michael Adams' booking to take two horses to Newmarket, asked to meet Adams for a drink in The Red Lion, just along the road from Monk's Lane Stables as he needed to speak to him on a business matter.

Agreeing to meet at eight o'clock, Adams was expecting Mullins to tell him that his fees were increasing and was prepared to refuse to accept any increase as things were already tight and he simply couldn't afford it.

After buying the drinks, unusual for Mullins, Adams was even more convinced of the reason for the meeting.

Looking around furtively and clearly uncomfortable, Mullins stressed the need for secrecy and the conversation they were about to have would be on a strictly confidential footing.
Mullins proceeded to confide in Adams his lucrative sideline and offered Adams a proposition that would net him thousands of pounds, tax-free. All he had to do was supply the horses to be entered at the meetings where he needed to send his transporters. That was his only involvement. He did not need to know why and who knows he may even pick up a bit of prize money if he sent the right horses.

With his marriage, seemingly in a downward spiral through lack of money, his next question settled Mullins' nerves,
"How many thousands?"
"That depends on the job, but I need a horse to run at Nimes on Arc Day and if that job is successful, then you're looking at £5000, but there will be plenty more where that came from", answered a much more confident Mullins.
"No involvement, just supply the horses? No risk? No comeback?"

"No, and the, err, let's call them expenses, will all be paid in cash so there will be no money trail plus I know, like me, it will help at home".

"We'd better meet for a drink when you need to give me the details, I don't want any phone records", whispered Adams.

"Great", beamed an ebullient Mullins, "I'll get us another round".

The racing at Nimes provided a good quality card and contained a valuable handicap for 3-year-olds, the Prix de Marseille with 18,000 euros in prize money on offer and Adams decided that he may as well try to pick up some prize money as well as his "expenses" and if he sent a winner, this would provide perfectly legitimate grounds for Mullins horsebox to carry whatever it was he was carrying, along with his horse, back to Abbot's Meadow.

Michael Adams had bought Monk's Lane Stables from a mediocre retiring trainer fifteen years ago and, whilst now a seemingly successful enterprise, with an almost full yard of 32 horses, his maximum capacity was 36, the costs of running the yard compared with the income from training fees meant the bottom line was scarcely break even, particularly as he had overstretched himself in developing the stables by building an additional twelve stable block to complement the original twenty-four.

The mortgage repayments on the house and yard were astronomical and increasing the training fees, already amongst the highest in the County, would surely mean his owners moving their assets away and tipping the business into losses if they couldn't be replaced.

He also knew from experience of watching other yards that once owners were found to be moving their horses away from a struggling stable, others would follow suit, like having a run on the bank when people panicked about the security of their savings, and this was something Adams simply couldn't risk.

He had overstretched himself attempting to compete with his famous father-in-law, encouraged and occasionally goaded by his avaricious wife Alexandra.

Alexandra was the daughter of Sir Anthony Marks, one of the most successful of British trainers at the prestigious Markham House stables in Newmarket. As such Alex had been accustomed to the best of everything, best cars, designer clothes, luxury travel and to spend the fifteen years of her marriage with little in the way of luxuries provided by Michael was a growing and almost fatal disappointment to her.

However, as the only child, her father always financed her luxurious lifestyle to the chagrin of her hard-working husband, until that is, Sir Anthony's death two years ago.

Although he left his only daughter well provided for, Alex had no intention of allowing Michael to get his hands on any of her inheritance.

After all, she justified to herself, their marriage had been increasingly difficult with financial constraints holding back her natural lifestyle and if daddy had had to provide for her whilst he was alive, who was going to do it now?

She wondered how long she would stay with Michael now that she had enough money of her own to start again anywhere she chose, and the thought of sipping cocktails on a Caribbean beach instead of freezing in this Godforsaken part of Yorkshire eight months of the year was an almost irresistible temptation.

Whilst her father doted on his daughter and had ensured she was very well provided for, her stepmother Corrine controlled the business after his death, as even Sir Anthony had realised that the business he had built from scratch, with years of dedication and pure hard work over almost thirty years, would probably be cursorily sold if he left it to Alex.

If he did, the knowledge that this would leave his loyal owners, who had not just in the main become friends but had provided all his wealth and reputation, having to find other homes for their horses, was something he refused to even contemplate.

Michael looked at the race conditions and chose his excellent, improving bay filly, Indian Summer who had won a 7-furlong maiden at Newbury last time out. Impressively coming from fifth entering the final furlong, the scarlet cap of jockey

Jamie Maxwell aboard the 12/1 chance had cruised up on the outside and had won by 2 lengths going away from a 15-runner field packed with promising horses, a couple of which had confirmed the form by winning since, and since this was her only win the odds on the Pari-Mutuel at Nimes should be good enough to win a few Euros on her as well.

Chapter 4

"Same place two o'clock?"
"OK".

This was the sum total of the stilted conversation between Michael Adams and Stella Mullins when Adams called to arrange their regular romantic rendezvous.
To be more precise it was a sexual rendezvous not romantic as both knew that there was no future in the relationship and neither wanted that anyway.
For Michael, the demanding Alexandra was demanding just luxuries and wealth, she had long ago stopped demanding sex. Their marriage was teetering on a knife edge and he knew that she would leave at the first opportunity and if he was honest with himself, he could not care one way or the other.
Stella, however, was simply insatiable.
Adams was fairly sure that he was not the only one who she was using to fulfil her needs but as she was fulfilling his, it was a pretty simple mutual arrangement.

Mullins was going with Adams' Head Lad Seamus Collins to Chester where Adams' had two runners entered on Ladies Day at the August Meeting. Greensleeves was in the 3.15pm Chester Stakes Listed Handicap and Silver Nymph, his promising 3-y-o colt, in the 4.20pm Handicap for horses rated 81 to 100 for which he just qualified, being currently rated 99! The bright, sunny and warm afternoon would firm up the already good to firm going and this would suit both horses.

Mullins was looking forward to relieving the bookmakers of a considerable amount as Adams and Collins were supremely confident of their entries as the tight, circular track at Chester always favoured horses that were drawn with a low number, meaning that they could stick to the rails, effectively running a shorter distance and being difficult to pass, and as Greensleeves was drawn one and Silver Nymph three in their respective races, optimism was high.

Mullins' love of racing and betting, combined with the qualified knowledge of Adams meant that he would go racing whenever he was able, leaving plenty of opportunities for Adams and Stella to enjoy themselves.

Their assignation place of choice was The Grouse and Hare pub just outside of Hutton-le-Hole, where they had three comfortable En-suite rooms, a tiny restaurant, and a discreet landlady, who never asked for any identification for Mr & Mrs. Smith of York when they checked in with no luggage and never staying for more than a couple of hours.

"Same place" was the Grouse, and at 2pm on an afternoon, even weekends, there would be just an occasional walking party in the bar, the locals having had their couple of pints at lunchtime and gone home for a nap.

Adams was waiting in the Car Park for Stella when she arrived in her Black Mercedes. Wearing her large sunglasses, which she always wore when they met but this time at least, it was enforced as the sun shone out of a clear azure sky, a short, pale-green dress with a low, square neckline showcasing her heavy, tanned breasts and black stiletto heels which accentuated her long, shapely legs. Her long, black wavy hair reached almost to the top of her shapely bottom and large, gold-hooped earrings framed her attractive tanned face with steel blue eyes. Adams was already aroused.

As they walked into the deserted bar, the knowing landlady, Coral, who had seen them arrive, laid the heavy, brass key to room 3 on the dark oak stained bar as Stella walked up the red carpeted stairs without even looking, they always had Room 3.

Adams locked the door behind them and turned to see Stella had dropped her dress to the floor and stood to face him naked.
He realised looking at the crumpled dress on the carpet and no other clothing in sight that she must have had nothing on underneath it.

An hour later, showered and dressed, they got into their respective cars and left for home.

This was a routine. No surprises, no promises, no expectations. They expected only to spend the time enjoying each other which they did vigorously and passionately until they were both satisfied. Nothing more, nothing less. That was what they agreed, that is how it had to be.

Their rendezvous, however, were getting more frequent and Adams was beginning to realise that he was only happy when either with Stella or looking forward to meeting her the next time.

As he drove home he thought about the afternoon and wondered just how long he would need to continue convincing himself that he could stick to their arrangement.
In the beginning, it was just fun. Great sex with the promise of more to come. Over time, however, he had wanted more. The sex had got better and more often and he knew from the intensity when they were making love that she felt it too. Maybe something would happen soon, or maybe he would have to make it.

When he arrived at the yard the lads were all smiling, both horses had won, Greensleeves by a length at 7/1 and Silver Nymph by a head at 9/1 and all the lads had won enough for their Saturday night out and then some.

Alexandra was as usual nowhere to be seen.
"Gone to Harrogate shopping", was the note on the hall table, with no time when she could be expected back. He cursed himself that he could have spent an extra hour with Stella, but he also knew that he could not have lasted another ten minutes never mind another hour, so instead thought about the afternoon's encounter and the two winners. They say that things come in three's, so he couldn't wait to see what the third was going to be!

Mullins delivered the winners back to the yard at eight-thirty that evening and it was left to Collins to put them into their stables, feeding and watering them as an unsuspecting, ebullient Mullins, who had won fifteen hundred pounds at Chester asked if Adams wanted to go for a pint at "The White Swan" at the side of Pickering Beck. He knew Adams' lads would be in the Margrave on a Saturday night so thought his own local would be more appropriate, but Adams declined, claiming that he was waiting for Alexandra to get back and they were having supper together at home. He had no idea where she was or even if she would be home tonight, and such was the state of their relationship, half of him hoped she wouldn't.

Mullins arrived home to Stella,
"There's an Indian in the oven. I've already eaten", she mumbled as she lay on the sofa watching a film on TV without looking up. He took one look at it and decided was not his type of film.
"Coming to the Pub?"
"No, you go if you want, I'm having an early night".
And with that, he got into his Jaguar and drove to a packed "White Swan" where he had a couple of pints and decided that after all he fancied the Indian to complement the Double Cheeseburger and Chips he had at the Races.
Waiting for the takeaway to warm through, he emptied his pockets and wallet and counted his winnings. One thousand, four hundred and eighty-seven pounds.

He put the cash in a brown envelope in the top drawer of the oak sideboard that they bought together when they first moved to Yorkshire. It had taken almost all their savings to buy it and it was now home to envelopes containing over thirty thousand pounds. Much as he hated banks, he knew that he would have to find a way of investing the money but Money Laundering Laws nowadays meant that it was impossible to do this, as banks and financial institutions were governed by strict regulations on the amount they could accept in cash.

This meant that the only schemes where he could invest cash were highly suspect, not governed by any legislation and therefore by nature, very high risk. "Maybe I'll look at it doing something with it soon", he promised himself, looking again at the huge amount of cash that for the first time in his life had been earned legitimately, well mainly.

After his supper, which he ate alone in front of the TV watching highlights of the Test Match against India, which England was again somehow trying hard to lose, and wishing that Stella had stayed up for him, he reminisced about the Saturday nights they used to have, when they would go out drinking and dancing from seven o'clock 'til late, then come home with a takeaway or kebab which they would demolish before having unadulterated sex on the sofa in front of the fire before collapsing shattered into bed and sleeping late on Sunday.

Nowadays it was a re-heated takeaway, watching cricket on his own and going to bed to marvel at the long, tanned back of his snoring wife.

Maybe it was him he thought, as he couldn't bring himself to find any fault with his wife who he still loved, and promising to try to do more to get back to the way things used to be, he pulled the lightweight summer duvet over him and went to sleep almost immediately.

Adams lay awake, thinking of Stella until he slept fitfully, being awoken by the front door banging and footsteps on the stairs, around three o'clock.
She must have slept in the spare room as he woke alone and went to watch the string on the gallops for morning work. He was amazed that the lads and work riders were always alert and up to the task despite their nights out whilst he had only had a disturbed night's sleep and was not his usual bright self, evident by the quiet morning instead of bellowing instructions to everyone.

Alexandra was still in bed when he returned and after he had cooked his own breakfast, Kippers from nearby Whitby was his Sunday morning treat, he was reading the Sunday Papers when a hung-over and bedraggled Alexandra put in an appearance.
"Good morning", she whispered heading straight for the coffee pot.
"What time did you get in?" he inquired.
"About twelve but you were asleep and I didn't want to wake you so I slept in the spare room". she lied.
"Buy anything nice?"
"No, I couldn't see anything", more lies.
She poured herself a black coffee and put a slice of wholemeal bread into the toaster, that was breakfast.
No wonder she kept her Covergirl figure he thought.

"I'm meeting Susannah for lunch, do you want to come?" she asked, not meeting his eyes.
"No, you go, I've got things to do here".

After putting his dishes in the dishwasher, he went to look at the horses, nothing else was spoken.
Illogically, he got into his Range Rover and went for a drive past Mullins Yard, hoping to catch a glimpse of Stella. He wished he hadn't, for he saw a giggling Stella standing at the back of one of the horseboxes with one of the drivers, Bălan, and the body language said there was obviously more than an employer / employee relationship.
Adams knew he had no right to expect anything from her, after all, they had both agreed at the outset that it was a no strings, just for fun relationship and he had agreed.
However, he was angry and jealous, whether he a right to be or not, and this on top of the state of his home life which this morning had typified, knew that something had to change.

Chapter 5

Ştefan Bălan, and his red-haired Irish co-driver
Connor McLaughlin pulled the immaculate and
distinctive burgundy and silver liveried transporter of
Mullins Transport into the wet, heavily puddled truck
park at Nimes at 4.30pm on the afternoon prior to
racing, with security consisting of just two uniformed
guards who had to make a real effort to come out
their sentry post.

The two drivers produced the required parking pass
and horse passport to the soulless security guards who
for the past two hours had ambled backwards and
forwards to raise the manual, counterbalanced red and
white chevron barrier with no protection from the
heavy downpour, which judging by the heavy, black
clouds, showed little sign of abating.

They joked about being warm and dry in their cab to
the sub-contracted guards who McLaughlin knew
from his previous trips to French racecourses, and
after less than even a cursory inspection drove
confidently through the now lifted steel barrier after
being told with growl in a heavy French accent to
fuck off!

They parked up some 500m away from the stable
block where Indian Summer would be prepared for
tomorrow's race, giving plenty of time for the filly to
rest after the journey.

Shortly after their arrival, a larger, navy blue four-horse transporter drew up alongside, the gold script lettering of Henri Duvall Racing standing out in the dismal, murky, late autumn afternoon light.

Henri Duvall was a successful and well-respected trainer with a yard on the outskirts of Les Pennes-Mirabeau, ideally situated close to the A7, A51, and A55 Autoroutes and just 20km from the bustling international port of Marseille.

Henri like most trainers had not always been successful and had worked for many years building up a yard nearer to Aix-en-Provence from the modest 20 horses which had been sufficient for his laid-back father who had settled for a comfortable lifestyle. His father was content to deal only with undemanding owners of modest means who were satisfied with the occasional winner and didn't threaten to remove horses if they didn't live up to expectations, relying on Henri Senior's judgement and honesty that sometimes their charges were simply not good enough, but "we may be able to find a little race here and there to go towards the costs and a nice day out with a glass of champagne or two".

Henri Junior, however, had different plans and after his father's death from cancer, even his father's loyal owners soon noticed a difference with their horses improving and winning in better quality races.

The increase in their prize money, whilst not increasing their overall wealth dramatically was nevertheless welcome and Henri became, over a five-year period something of a fashionable trainer, attracting wealthier owners and better horses, but at a price.

He moved to the bigger yard in Les Pennes-Mirabeau, bought from a retiring trainer and subsequently took on more costs and acquired less forgiving owners, although so far the last three years had been successful with several notable horses including Harvest Moon, winner of the French 2000gns and a creditable third in the Arc de Triomphe itself and Miracle Worker, winner of the Irish 1000gns.

Henri's proudest moments however were his marriage to Camille, his girlfriend from school and the birth of their child, Elise.

What Henri did not know, and Camille would never know, at that time was that threats to Elise's life would be used to ensure his involvement in the smuggling, gun running and trafficking operations controlled by the Rumanian Mafia which although he was a most unwilling partner was quite lucrative.

The interiors of the two transporters whilst different sizes were the same design and built by the same coachbuilder to provide the same secure, self - contained compartments capable of storing a variety of illegal cargoes in complete secrecy, including people.

Mullins Transport was a familiar sight at most of the racecourses around Europe and on either their arrival or departure, their drivers were well trained to be over-helpful and friendly with any security personnel on their first few legitimate visits, using the rapport built to ensure that when they passed through racecourse entrances at a busy time, which was the result of meticulous planning, they were usually waved through with at worst a scant inspection.

Bălan and McLaughlin unloaded Indian Summer and settled her into stable number 106, ensuring that she had water and the special feed mix they had taken with them from Abbot's Meadow. Once installed safely, her security was the responsibility of the racecourse security staff who were present and they returned to the truck.

After McLaughlin had collected three large bags of food and several litre bottles of Pepsi from Speed Rabbit Pizzas, just half a mile from the course, whilst Bălan remained in the truck, they climbed up into their quarters for the night, closing the blackout cab curtains and turning on the small portable TV precariously balanced on top of the dashboard.

Henri's drivers Pierre and Jean similarly unloaded their three charges before returning to their truck with buckets of Kentucky Fried Chicken and Fries.

At 2am precisely, McLaughlin lifted the bottom bunk bed forward and proceeded to remove the lower back plate of the cab as Bălan peeked out from the darkened cab across to Duvall's transporter and watched Pierre, dressed in black jeans and fleece, climb silently from the heavily curtained cab before stretching and looking all around to ensure that he was not observed and that everyone was asleep. Satisfied that the shadows of the two trucks would conceal any activity should the moon make an unexpected appearance and that he was the only one around, he put his hand up to Bălan who stepped carefully and quietly from the cab, satisfying himself that they were alone.

The four girls that were helped down by Pierre looked stiff and frightened as they were shepherded across the short space and helped into Mullins truck and immediately housed in the concealed compartment.

The girls ate in silence, devouring the pizzas provided by McLaughlin, as this was their first meal since 10 o'clock that morning.

Showing his newly acquired cargo the Glock 380 handgun concealed in his waistband, he ensured that the girls understood the need to keep concealed and the consequences if not, speaking to them in their native Rumanian to confirm the arrangement for further reassurance.

They were told that there was enough food and drink already stored in the overhead bins to keep them fed and watered for the next 24 hours but to use this sparingly as they would not be able to leave their "security cabin" for at least that period, by which time they would be in the UK and ready for their new "careers" before McLaughlin refitted the panel and retired to his bunk.

The girls, all aged between 17 and 22, had been promised a variety of positions in the UK where they would earn sufficient money to make a new life for themselves and be able to send money back to Rumania every week to ensure that their loved ones escaped the appalling poverty endured by many thousands of Rumanian families.

Raceday started with a bright, cloudless sky but with an uncharacteristic chill in the morning air after yesterday's heavy rain.

Yawning from his disturbed night's sleep, McLaughlin went in search of bacon baguettes and fresh coffee from the on-course cafe. The thrill of the afternoon to come was manifested in the atmosphere of the waiting queue and listening to almost exclusively French accents and the seemingly good-natured banter of the stable hands, the excited conversation was all about prospects in the Arc, not of their charges at Nimes.

Distancing himself as much as possible from the operation Adams took one of his stable lads Allan Parsons to Warwick where he had entered three runners at the afternoon's televised meeting, he would be sure to make himself as visible as possible which should not be too difficult as he fancied at least one horse of his horses, Sunset Beach, to win and as the owner was a famous actor was sure to hog the limelight if she won.

This left Mullins driver to take care of Indian Summer, which although not ideal was not that unusual as it wasn't possible to be at every meeting with every horse.

The official going was good, yesterday's rain coming after a couple of dry, windy days but French jockey Martine Deneuve, engaged to ride for Adams for the first time as stable jockey Jamie Maxwell was booked to ride at Warwick, walked the course to find the best racing side for Summer as she liked going as firm as possible and it was this attention to detail that could make the difference between winning and being an also-ran, with the resulting loss of potential income.

Deciding the stand side rail was the best route she would follow Adams instructions to tuck her in behind the leaders until the last furlong before giving her daylight and go light on the whip as she doesn't respond too well to it.

Even when speaking to the pintsize Martine on the phone, in the back of his mind was the knowledge that whatever happened today it was a tax-free £5,000 payday, but Adams wanted the share of the prize money too and having seen Summer at Newbury, thought that this was a real possibility.

Adams met Allan Parsons as he walked a spirited Sunset Beach into the Parade Ring. Stable jockey Jamie Maxwell wearing the instantly identifiable colours of the silver-grey jacket with scarlet cross belts and cap and with the number 7 saddle cloth, would it be lucky? walked in with the other fifteen jockeys to receive a leg up on to his eager charge.

With eager anticipation, the horses were loaded into the starting stalls and they were off, Sunset Beach sitting comfortably on the rails in sixth place where she stayed until passing the two-furlong marker when Jamie moved her out to give her a clear run as he sensed the horse in front of him, a grey filly named Stockholm, was beginning to tire.
Seeing daylight in front of her Sunset wanted to make her run and had to be held up as Jamie knew that once she hit the front she would lose concentration.
Her ears pricked as she heard the roar from the stands as they passed the furlong marker and Jamie asked for her effort giving her a light tap with the whip to keep her focused, she felt to be moving easily and the owner was shouting at the top of her voice as she got her nose in front just 100 metres from the post but the second horse, the fast finishing Cloudy Bay, kept fighting and they passed the post together, a photo-finish.

Neither jockey was confident enough to go into the winners' berth in the enclosure before the judge's announcement, walking their steaming, sweating excited mounts around in circles in mounting suspense amid the hullabaloo.

The loudspeakers crackled into life, first number 7, second number 1, third number 12. Jamie steered Sunset into the winner's spot and dismounted to hugs and kisses from Charmaine Jones, the wealthy actor owner, standing right next to her trainer as the TV presenter interviewed first Jamie and an excited Charmaine.

Adams was confident that he could not have had a more visible alibi should anything go wrong.

In contrast, Bălan was trying to take a nap as McLaughlin walked Indian Summer from the saddling enclosure before giving Martine a leg up into the saddle.

The race, however, was every bit as exciting as the racegoers who dragged themselves away from the racing at Longchamps which was being shown on large TV screens in the bars, were treated to a neck and neck last furlong with first Indian Summer and then Cote d'Azure got their head in front only for the other horse to fight back and there was nothing to choose between them as they passed the post, with merely a murmur coming from the expectant crowd when the judge announced that Martine had got Indian Summer up to beat the hot favourite and win by a nose.

Unsaddling his charge, McLaughlin raced to get Summer loaded into the horsebox as they were intent on leaving the course at the earliest opportunity and would not stop until the rendezvous to unload the girls just off the A1M near Doncaster.

Three-quarters of an hour later, the excitement of the win fading and the with the knowledge of the job in hand, Bălan eased the transporter out of Nimes onto the A9 towards Orange and Lyon and headed for home, careful to adhere to all traffic signs and speed limits, after all the last thing they needed now was to be stopped by the French Police.

Arriving in Dover at 12.30am, they drove straight through customs as was predicted at this time on a dark Monday morning and made their journey northwards on the A20, M25, and A1 to deliver the consignment.

Chapter 6

Four-thirty on a cold, dark, wet and windy Monday morning in October was the middle of the night and most people were safely under, warm duvets in the comfort of their beds.

The only traffic on the arterial roads was the overnight trucks who chose early starts to deliver goods to meet timed morning delivery schedules and the businessmen who started early for first appointments in other parts of the country and who didn't want their business to interfere with their family weekends.

The roads were quiet.

Bălan pulled the transporter off the A1M at Blyth Services and onto the deserted A614 Bawtry Road just south of Doncaster.

Two Mercedes, a sleek, black E220 estate car with blacked out windows and a powerful, silver four-wheel drive M330, were waiting in the unlit lay-by just half a mile away.

With the development of the new Service Area with its floodlit canopy illuminating twelve pumps and the accompanying modern, budget priced Travelodge, the lay-by was scarcely used in the daytime never mind at this time of the morning as it meant trucks pulling off the motorway and the risk to the drivers and their cargoes of parking overnight in such a lonely spot were far too great and drivers instead drove onto Markham Moor Truck Stop just twelve miles further south where they could use showers and have a cooked meal instead of eating in their cabs.

As Bălan pulled in behind the cars, McLaughlin began to remove the seating and the back panel of the cab to release the girls, who were woken by the lurch of the transporter as the hiss of the air brakes brought it to a halt.

Greeting the driver of the Mercedes estate car nearest to him, who he knew previously from his time in Bucharest, Bălan opened the front of his worn, brown leather bomber jacket to display his Austrian-made 9mm Glock handgun.

The driver Alex laughed deeply and using the remote control to open the tailgate of the sinister estate car turned to collect a battered green and beige holdall from the boot hidden by his long, leather coat. Having retrieved it he turned to see that Bălan had both hands on his gun which was aimed straight at him. "Quite right my friend, trust no-one" he chuckled, "especially your friends".

Taking the holdall, Bălan unzipped the top to reveal the contents before signaling to McLaughlin to unload the girls, who stumbled stiffly out of the cab and staggered, huddled together in fear and shivering in the cold towards the man in the leather coat who now held a pistol in his right hand.

Inspecting the girls and selecting Petra, a petite, short-haired blonde who looked no more than fifteen and Chloe, a buxom curly-haired brunette who was the only one of the four who appeared to have attitude.

He held open the rear door of the estate car whilst the rear door of the four-by-four opened and a shaven headed thug covered in tattoos held this open for the remaining, whimpering girls.

Alex spoke in their native Rumanian "Bine ai venit, intra si eu te voi duce la noile case" "Welcome to England, get in and we'll take you to your new homes".

Leaving little doubt in the terrified girl's minds of the meaning behind the smiled greeting, reinforced, as if this was necessary, by the brandished weapon and the certain consequences of trying to escape, he shepherded the girls towards the waiting cars.
Alex was joined by another armed associate, Sean, an Irishman in his early twenties with curly ginger hair, his heavily freckled face giving the impression of someone even younger, in the front of the estate car and locked the doors, before both cars sped off with a screech of tyres, drowning the cries from their passengers.

McLaughlin watched as the two Mercedes sped away with their merchandise, Bălan remaining stationary, his hands remaining steady on his weapon and the holdall at his feet until they were out of sight.
"Know them, did you?" inquired McLaughlin once he had turned the transporter around and they were back on the motorway travelling north.
"I knew the guy with the cash, Alex, when I was young, very nasty person, doesn't need to be paid to hurt people, he enjoys it. Be very careful if you ever meet him again, bad news."

They drove in silence as Bălan counted the cash, £100,000 in used notes of all denominations. "Good days work my friend, now home for some sleep", as he closed his eyes and left his colleague to get them back to Abbot's Meadow.

Sleep was not something that would be coming anytime soon for the girls, as the estate car drove the short journey to Sheffield in the miserable, pitch black morning, the four-by-four driving over the A628 Woodhead Pass, which was as usual at this time of year shrouded in fog, carrying on towards Manchester.

Sean pulled the estate car around the back of a row of buildings, the headlights illuminating overflowing tall red plastic dustbins and disturbing a pair of cats searching for scraps of food.
Taking a large bunch of keys from his jacket pocket he quickly opened a door at the top of two filthy concrete steps, before Alex opened the car door and ushered the girls inside. Climbing a staircase of stained, bare wood whose sides had long ago been painted cream when they had presumably been covered in a stair carpet, they looked even dirtier at this time of the morning being lit by a single lightbulb hanging from an old twisted flex on the landing at the top, where five doors were all secured by padlocks to the outside.

Terrified of just what would greet them behind the doors, Sean unlocked the furthest door on the right and with the armed Alex at the rear, pushed the girls into the room.

The room was lit with the orange glow of the street lighting outside and the cold, damp room contained two mattresses on the floor with various unwashed crumpled bed linen strewn on top of it and ominously the windows were barred on the outside making an escape from this nightmare impossible, there was no way out.

On the far wall was a wash basin and toilet, and under the barred window was a small dilapidated dressing table covered in make-up and lipsticks, whilst on the wall to the left was the carcass of a wardrobe, the front now covered with a dirty floral fabric curtain on a plastic covered wire.

As the two girls, cold, hungry and scared, heard the steel bolt slide across and the heavy clunk as the brass padlock snapped closed, a voice called out from the pile of bedclothes on the mattress nearest to the window "for God's sake be quiet some of us have only just got to bed".

Chloe, now holding Petra tightly tried to stop the sobs that racked her tiny body. Finding the other mattress was unoccupied they lay down and covered themselves with the spare bedding and eventually fell into a restless sleep.

They awoke the following morning to the sounds of a toilet flushing and a radio playing. The voices of the girls with whom they had shared the room spoke in Rumanian.

"More competitions arrived, wonder how long they will last?" the deep guttural voice of the short-haired brunette nearest the window asked of a pretty blonde with long flowing curls and an hour glass figure, complete with make-up which would have been over the top but attractive last night but this morning was smudged and made her look like a tramp.

"Rumanian?" Anna, the brunette, asked of the stirring Chloe.
"Yes, we were promised jobs not this, how do we get out of here?"
"You don't, well not alive. Two girls have tried before and never been found, so take some advice, suck up to the bodyguards and they will look after you with food and goodies but whatever happens, you will need to give them and the customers just what they want, if not", Anna made a slashing gesture with her hand across her throat.

Chloe and Petra were to learn just what was expected and the consequences of not doing what they were told.

Most of the girls who arrived at Veronica's were immediately intimidated by the doormen who effectively managed the operations.
Most of the girls were terrified and threatened with violence and it was common for a new arrival to be beaten in front of the others to make sure there were no misunderstandings from day one.

Chloe, however, was different.

She had an attitude that made others think that she was in charge and it was the doormen who worked for her.

Of course, she did favours for them but she was very popular with the clients, more than a few becoming regulars and only asking for her by name. This gave her status amongst the girls and more of a free reign with the doormen who concentrated on managing the others.
This also meant that she used the extra freedom if that's what it could be called, to try to plot her way out of this hell hole.

Chapter 7

Patrick awoke to an inky, threatening sky with dark clouds promising rain. He must have slept in, very unusual for him, and wondered why he could hear Chris Evans' Morning Show and smell bacon frying. He looked at his watch on the bedside table, 7.45am, what was Mrs. Weston doing here on a Tuesday and at this time?

He dressed and went downstairs without showering to find his breakfast of bacon, sausages and tomatoes warming in the AGA and Mrs. Weston looking at the coffee machine as if it was a time machine.
"Let me show you", he exclaimed, startling the humming Mrs. Weston.
"Do you always creep around, I never heard you get up".
"It pays sometimes", he joked.
He demonstrated just how easy it was to work the machine, one of the things he liked most about it and put a carefully measured scoop of his best-loved Santos beans in to grind and brew.
"I usually only have croissants for breakfast, a Full English is a special Sunday morning treat. Anyway, what are you doing here at this time and on a Tuesday?"
"Alan", Mr. Weston was an HGV driver for a firm in Northallerton delivering pigs to slaughterhouses nationwide, "had to go to Nottingham this morning early and this place needs a good clean now that you've unpacked, so that I can keep on top of it, don't worry I won't charge you extra!"

"No, I'm happy to pay you, anyway that bacon smells delicious, I don't suppose we have any eggs"

"Plenty, sunny side up?"

Breakfast was a treat and Mrs. Weston was turning out to be a gem, things were looking very promising.

The removal van arrived around 10am just after Patrick had left for the village store to pick up his morning paper and they had cleared the outbuildings and left before he returned, much to Patrick's delight. This meant that he could now arrange the transfer of the horses and whilst they would not be there for this weekend, Melanie would be, and he couldn't wait to see her and walk her around the 22-acre farm which he still had to decide what to do with.

Did he rent the fields to one of the other farms? Find a tenant farmer to work the land? Start his own stables or stud farm? He had not had time to seriously consider any of these options but it felt strange that he now had the funds to do whatever he wanted, maybe this would make it a more difficult choice?

Julie called shortly before lunch, "I've arranged for the stables to be cleared on Friday, sorry I couldn't sort it any earlier".

"Sorry?"

"The van will be there on Friday to clear the stables like you asked".

"The van came this morning; it's all been taken. They had all the paperwork, they left me a copy, can you please check that they were your people and call me straight back?"

Alarm bells were ringing, if they weren't the one's organised by Julie, who were they and why did they take all the risk for a stable full of average furniture? None of it had seemed to be antique or valuable, in fact even the Persian Carpet which he assumed had been in the lounge because of its size was not genuine and worth at best a hundred and fifty quid, so what had been in there?

His mobile rang a few moments later. "Hello Mr Spencer, it wasn't Wainwright's, they know nothing about it so you'll need to contact the Police and let them know that it's been stolen".

Three hours later, the lack of bodies and the size of the rural area covered, meant that the Police response was greatly different to that he was used to in Manchester, a grey Mitsubishi L200 Police vehicle with fluorescent blue and yellow stripes ambled into the farm yard. Strangely the first thought that came into his mind was that he should get a dog, not just for the early warning system but he'd had a dog, a Labrador called Jess, when he was boy on the family farm just outside of Malton and had never been able to have another as his police career, given he was single, meant that it just wasn't practical.

DC Heather Miller, ambitious and newly promoted to CID, was a slim built 23-year-old with shoulder-length dark brown hair and wearing brown high heels, tan trousers and a dark brown tailored jacket over a gold shirt, very autumnal thought Patrick, and accompanied by DC Jason Crowe carefully approached the house.

DC Crowe was tall, over 6 feet and sporting designer stubble, to Patrick he simply looked unshaven and wore a charcoal three-piece suit and tan shoes. Patrick could never accept this combination, however fashionable it was, as being somehow correct, a grey suit should have black shoes!

Crowe had been in CID for 5 years, was due to take his sergeant exams in a couple of months and displayed a bored, seen it all before, just routine attitude which irritated Patrick within the first 5 seconds. Whether it was his languid walk, his unkempt appearance or waiting for his partner to make the introductions he was unsure, but irritated he was.

Once Heather had introduced the pair and shown their warrant cards they walked into the kitchen and pulled up heavy chairs at the oak refectory table which Patrick had brought with him from Cheshire. It always seemed out of place in his flat but seemed to compliment his new kitchen perfectly.

"So what's missing?" said DC Crowe

"I really couldn't tell you, the van came to clear the stables of all the furniture and stuff the previous owner left behind, so he would know better than me, I never really looked in there".

"If they were not the one's that the agent arranged, how did they know to collect the stuff and when the real firm was scheduled to collect it? It seems a bit of a risk wouldn't you say?"

"I would say yes, but even more worrying is that they had all the right paperwork, my name, the previous owner's name, Novotny, the agent's name and the company name on the paperwork which matched the van. They even gave me a receipt and copy of the collection sheet to keep, I'll get them for you".

"Can you describe the men for us?" asked Crowe

"As I told you that I was in the village at the time that seems unlikely, doesn't it?" said an increasingly irritated Patrick, would he have responded that way if Heather had asked the question? "But you could ask Mrs. Weston, she was here at the time".

Mrs. Weston then proceeded to describe the driver and his helper in great detail and the officers thought they recognised the professional attention to detail of a colleague.

"Were you ever in the force Mrs. Weston?" said Crowe looking a little more interested.

"I was a WPC with North Yorkshire Police until I got married, but they didn't like married women who wanted families back then". Patrick could hardly disguise his surprise as Mrs. Weston smiled at him.

"Some things never change," said Heather with something of a knowing look in her eye.

"It must be someone at the agents or Wainwright's that tipped them off, so I suggest that maybe the place to start", pronounced Patrick impatiently.

"With respect Mr. Spencer, we'll handle the enquiry now and be in touch with you if we need anything else," said Crowe superciliously.

"Did you by any chance see a dark grey Discovery with blacked out windows on your way here?" asked Patrick.

"Lots of Land Rovers around here sir, it comes with the territory," replied Crowe, closing his notebook and getting up to leave.

His colleague looked a little uncomfortable when leaving and Patrick thought that she out of the two would probably make some enquiries, he was fairly sure that Crowe would rather just finish his shift.

As there were no further sightings of the Discovery for the rest of the week it looked as though the car was simply scouting for the opportunity to steal the contents of the stable, but it still didn't explain how they knew either what was in there or that the real removal van was booked for Friday.

He would need to find out even if Crowe wouldn't.

Chapter 8

Friday arrived with gale force winds and torrential rain and the forecast worsening, typical of the type of autumn days sent to clear the trees of all the beautiful colours of nature before the shortening days, dark nights and plummeting temperatures descended, seemingly turning autumn into winter overnight. Melanie was due to arrive at 7pm and although Patrick knew that she was an excellent driver, occasionally she had driven his Range Rover when they had been out together and he had fancied a drink, he still worried about her driving in these conditions, particularly in her small, red Audi TT convertible as he believed the bigger the car, the safer it was, learned from his early experiences in the force.

He knew she loved her Audi with her distinctive number plate, MAK77, Melanie Annelise Karlsonn and she had told him that she thought that 77 was as near as she could get to TT in numbers.

However, he wished she would get a bigger car, preferably some 4-wheel drive as she would be driving here most weekends and this would be far better suited to the countryside conditions in North Yorkshire. After all, everyone drove one for the school runs in Alderley Edge where seemingly children could not be driven anywhere in a normal car in case there was sudden heavy fall of snow on the way to or from school in June. Stop being cynical Patrick, he reprimanded himself!

He had planned a perfect night when she arrived. He had put fresh flowers on the table, there was a bottle of Chateauneuf du Pape ready to be opened, 2 juicy fillet steaks and a New York Baked Cheesecake with fresh raspberries and whipped cream topped with toasted almonds, her favourite dessert, in the large American style fridge which had kindly been left by the previous owner.

He had managed to find a fabulous shop, The Black Bull Farm Shop, in the next village which sold all their own home produced meats, had a great delicatessen and ready-made desserts to die for, which looking at the cholesterol content could be anytime soon.

The wood burning stove in the lounge was roaring away (after he managed to light it) with a pile of logs from the almost fully stocked log store and he had warm, soft, fluffy white towels waiting for her on the hot, chrome towel rail in the spacious bathroom. Though she hadn't even arrived yet, he almost couldn't wait for this perfectly planned evening to conclude as the thought of making love with Melanie again and feeling her warm, curvy, firm, fragrant body next to him in bed for the whole weekend almost made him forget about the strange events of the week, almost that is.

She had called when leaving the studio in Manchester and told him that her Satnav said she should be there for 6.30pm, but they both knew just how dreadful the traffic usually was on the M61 and M62 particularly on Friday afternoons with commuters leaving Manchester and Leeds early and parents collecting children from school, so she would try to call when she was a bit nearer.

They had also decided when he first bought the farm that her tastes in furnishings were far more sophisticated than his and she was looking forward to designing his new home. Did he think that she would be choosing for him or them as a couple?
The weekend would be idyllic and he planned to try to find a really good restaurant for Saturday night with which to impress her, although with a choice of eating in Alderley Edge and their love of La Scala it would need to be something special.
He called Julie at Oswald's on his mobile as the phone line and broadband was still not up and running to see if there were any very good restaurants within a reasonable distance.
She recommended two within just 15 miles, The Farriers in Malton and the Le Pomme D'Or in Helmsley which had one and two Michelin Stars respectively.

Opting for the best, he had managed to book Le Pomme D'Or for Saturday at 8.00pm only managing to get a table on a cancellation, the restaurant calling back just ten minutes after the receptionist Amanda telling him in a supercilious manner that they were fully booked.

For Saturday nights "it is advisable to book at least 4 months in advance sir".

When he told her that four months ago he had no idea that he would be living in this part of the country but as he was now a best-selling author, maybe she had read his book? and had moved nearby then he would be a regular diner.

He had to admit to being genuinely surprised when she told him yes she had actually read his book and looked forward to the next one.

When Amanda rang back she also asked if he would sign it for her? No problem, he told her with a smile knowing that in future he would probably be able to book whenever he wanted.

His mobile rang at 6.15pm and he answered fully expecting it to be Melanie.

"Where is it?" asked the muffled voice.

"Where's what and who is this?"

"Never mind who it is, we know that you have it, you have 48 hours to deliver it, we'll send you details of where. Very lonely on the Moors this time of year, wouldn't want to be out alone!"

"I've no idea what you're talking about", Patrick barked into the dead phone.

Just what did they want and how did they know about Melanie visiting? for the threat was obviously a direct one.

Before he could give any more thought to his next move his mobile rang again "I'll be there in 10 minutes älskling".

"Please be careful and don't stop for anything".

"What's wrong?" noting the anxious tone in his voice.

"Nothing, I just can't wait to see you", he lied.

Twenty minutes later he heard her car crunch on the graveled yard and strode out purposefully to greet her looking around for any unannounced guests.
Hurrying her inside he told her of the phone call and tried to work out how they seemed to know so much about what was happening with his life and the farm. It seemed incredulous but could the house be bugged and if so how and why?

Was it Patrick they were trying to scare or was this somehow related to the previous owner Novotny? Too many things were beginning to build a picture, the easy sale negotiation and fast completion, the office and stable security, the audacious theft of the stable contents and now the phone threat.
He knew that he would need to find out what it was all about and who was responsible, but he was determined nothing was going to spoil this first weekend in his new home with Melanie.

She came down from her bath wearing Patrick's bathrobe with wet hair and smelling of Estee Lauder Beautiful, which was most appropriate.
Patrick poured her a glass of wine which he had opened 20 minutes earlier to allow it to breathe whilst she toweled her hair by the roaring fire.
Curling up on the long sofa she looked so desirable that he wanted her there and then but knew she hadn't eaten since before lunchtime and if they made love now they may not want to eat at all tonight, so, desperately trying to be patient he put the steaks on to grill, medium for her, rare for him, to go with the fresh salad ready in the fridge.

The steak was as tender as the butcher at the farm shop had promised and they ate supper without speaking.

"What's for afters," she asked.
"That depends on you, or I have your favourite cheesecake?"
"Steady tiger, a girl needs to eat", she replied with a seductive laugh.

After dinner, Patrick insisted on filling the dishwasher, was he turning house-proud? before turning off the lights and putting her favourite Katie Melua album on low.
Sitting snugly with Melanie, watching the flames crackle and feeling the warmth of the fire and the wine, he tugged at the tied belt on her robe which fell open to expose her wonderfully curvy body and kissed her passionately, his firm hands caressing her warm soft body before she whispered in his ear "ta mig till sängs" (take me to bed).
He carried her up to his bedroom and knew just why he had been increasingly thinking about spending the rest of his life with her as they gorged their passions until they climaxed together, lying in each other's arms, content, sated and very much in love.

He woke her on the Saturday morning at 9.30am, lovely to have a lie-in after such a wonderful night.

He carried a breakfast tray of warm croissants and home-made strawberry jam (homemade by a lady in the village he was told), a boiled egg with hot buttered toast and a pot of fresh coffee with a small bone china cream jug with fresh double cream bought from the village shop but sourced from a local dairy farm. She loved cream in her coffee whilst he took his black.

"Breakfast darling," he said drawing back the curtains to let in the unseasonal autumn sunshine, yesterday's winds, having denuded many of the trees of the last vestiges of their foliage for the year, now being hardly a breeze.

"I'll show you around the farm and then we can take a walk into the village for a paper and some more eggs."

He kissed her warmly on the lips and wondered how anyone could look so beautiful when they awoke even with her hair being just a mass of tousled blonde curls.

He left her to breakfast and shower whilst he thought again about the strange events and the phone call. If the house was bugged it was a very professional job as he had spent an hour early this morning trying to find how to no avail and if someone was intent on finding out his movements and listening to his conversations, maybe they should have been more discreet last night. But this was his home and he would not be intimidated.

She came down wearing old, worn denim jeans and a big, navy, cable knit sweater over a plain white shirt with the collar standing up, wearing just a small amount of make-up and pale pink lipstick, smelling of the fresh Honeysuckle blossoms of Chevrefeuille by Yves Rocher, inexpensive perfume but one of her favourites for day wear and she knew it was also his.

Looking stunning until by contrast he noticed that she had odd socks on, one navy with white hearts and one plain ecru. "Don't laugh", she said sheepishly, "I packed in a hurry but as I'll have my Hunters on today no one will see them".
"You can always borrow some of mine", he laughed, but as he took a size 10 and she wore a size 4 he thought that hers may be better hidden in her Wellingtons.

Before donning wax jackets, he gave her a guided tour of the house as they were so intense last night she only saw part of the sprawling farmhouse. They went out into the fresh autumn air under gathering dark clouds to look at the outbuildings. "These stables will be fantastic for Torpedo and Borea and as you'll be here to look after them every day they'll get some real exercise. What do you want to do with the other spare ones?"
"I haven't had time to think about it really, don't forget that I have a book to write and Giles is going to be hassling me soon to find out how it's coming on, but with the royalties flooding in, we can do pretty much what we decide." Only after he said it did he realise that it was "we" and not the "I" that it would have naturally been just a few months ago.

As they walked around the fields that he now owned, he admitted to being surprised just how much land there was and it was close to lunchtime when they arrived in Abbot's Meadow to buy the paper and eggs from the Village Post Office.

Saturday mornings appeared to be a busy time and in typical village manner the conversation stopped as the customers turned to look at the new inhabitants.

"Morning both," said Michael Lampeter the Post Master breaking the spell, "Hope you find everything you want? If not let me know and we'll see if we can get it for you".

"Thanks, I will", replied Patrick.

Looking around the shop, Michael's wife Annabelle, who was considerably younger than her schoolmasterly husband and first impressions were that she had a far more vivacious personality with her shoulder length dark brown bob and petite frame seemingly full of vitality and bounce, made a point of introducing herself to Melanie.

"I'm Annabelle, hope you're settling in and we'll see more of you?"

"I'm Melanie, but actually I'm only visiting at weekends, Patrick's the one who's living here"

"Oops sorry, jumping to conclusions, again!" she replied embarrassingly, " Don't I know you from somewhere?"

Although Melanie had a regular show on BBC Radio4, because of her looks she occasionally appeared on TV, usually daytime or late night, but having once appeared on the cover of Radio Times when she first got the job presenting "A Good Read", meant that a lot of people knew her face but couldn't quite place her.

"I don't think so but you may have seen me on TV though, I'm a presenter on Radio 4".
"Wow, it' s nice to have a celebrity staying with us".
"Annabelle, Mrs. Warburton wants to pay her paper bill". Angela was in sole charge of the newspapers as she was the one able to be up at 5am including Sundays to sort out the deliveries without the need for an alarm clock.
Patrick had debated whether to have his paper delivered but thought the morning walk, almost a mile each way, was a good way to start the day and get the creative juices flowing, even better if he needed to exercise a dog, which was something that he had been considering as he thought this would fill the home when Melanie was in Manchester during the week.

Having bought his Telegraph and eggs, he decided to treat Melanie to the joys of the village pubs.
The Margrave was quiet, as you would expect on a Saturday lunchtime with all the stables having runners around the country but they ordered a pint of Black Sheep and a glass of Sauvignon Blanc from Angela, who took in every inch of Patrick's partner whilst being the perfect host, and took their seats next to the log fire which was blazing and hospitable even though there were few customers to enjoy it.

Patrick asked if she would like to wander across to The Red Lion for lunch but Melanie suggested another drink and back home for a sandwich and a "cosy afternoon" as they were booked into Le Pomme D'Or that evening and didn't think she could eat another meal and anyway she wanted to spend time together, hopefully in bed thought Patrick?

Strange that in all the times they had slept together in Cheshire and the holidays they had managed to take together in Italy and Sweden he had never felt this way. He just couldn't get enough of her and wondered whether it was the change of circumstance or scenery or was it a change of the intensity of his feelings for her. He thought he knew and hoped she felt the same way.

Before they went through the gates to the farm he stopped her abruptly. "Wait here." Looking cautiously around he walked slowly to the front door to which he had seen a white envelope pinned. He was undecided whether to take it down and read it or call Crowe and Miller, the rapid response crime fighting duo. Calling to Melanie to come he took the envelope down and they entered the house.

"Sunday, 9.00pm, leaf in the waste bin on Village Green" the note was handwritten in black ballpoint, all in upper case and wrongly spelled, he assumed correctly that they meant "leave".

The two things he had a problem with was first, he had no idea what he was supposed to leave and secondly even if he had, there was no way he would have given in to threats.

He had a day to decide what to do and as Melanie was driving back to Cheshire tomorrow afternoon he could at least be reasonably sure that he would be able to act alone, without the complication of worrying about her safety.

Chapter 9

Le Pomme D'Or turned out to be all that he had hoped for and more.

Situated in the picturesque Market Square in the lovely market town of Helmsley and just a relaxing 30 minutes' drive from Abbot's Meadow, the converted 18th Century Coaching Inn exuded the feel of quality even before they stepped out of the car. The frontage was beautifully lit, the signage reflected the status and the 4 AA Stars and host of other plaques mounted in an impressive column beside the door demonstrated that diners should feel confident of the quality to match this now heightened level of expectation.

Stepping into the reception area onto deep burgundy carpet with gold Fleur-de-Lys and being greeted by a smiling, friendly, late thirties, Head Waiter, impeccably dressed in an immaculate black suit with pristine white shirt and real black bow-tie, Patrick was welcomed by name and was very impressed, especially as this was his first visit.

Led into the bar area to study their burgundy and gold calf leather bound menus, Patrick ordered Tonic water with ice and lemon, as he was driving, and a Peach Bellini for Melanie.

Patrick ordered a fresh Whitby dressed crab for a starter, he was a lover of seafood and he thought it should be fresh having been caught just over 30 miles away.

Melanie chose Field Mushrooms on sourdough toast topped with a soft poached duck egg. The menu was so comprehensive and varied they had trouble choosing, but Patrick eventually selected Rack of Moors Bred Lamb with Creamed Potato and Tomato, Green Olive & White Bean Jus, Melanie preferring Pan Fried Sea Bass with Braised Fennel, Saffron & Shellfish Bisque.

They were shown to an intimate corner table in a very busy room although the volume of noise was little more than a hum and the waitresses in all burgundy uniforms with gold motifs were barely noticeable as they served discreetly and professionally.

Choosing a bottle of Chablis and iced, still water, having eyes only for each other across their candle lit table, they waited excitedly for a meal that didn't disappoint.

A few tables away to his right, Patrick saw a face that he recognised and was certain that it was Dan Ryan. Detective Sergeant Daniel Ryan to give him his full title. Patrick and Dan had worked together for three years on the Serious and Organised Crime Squad at the Met before his transfer to Greater Manchester Police and at one time they had become drinking buddies. Dan was a six feet tall, black athlete who could outrun anyone on the team at that time and he looked as though he was still in great shape, but what was he doing in a restaurant in North Yorkshire?

As Dan and his partner, an Asian girl who was dwarfed at his side, got up to leave, Patrick excused his self and strode over to greet him.

"Dan, what are you doing in here?"

"Patrick, what a surprise, this is my wife Nayna. I got transferred to North Yorks as a DI a couple of years ago. Look finish your meal and let's have a drink in the bar, we're in no hurry, we'll wait for you", he said waving to Melanie.

Returning to the table he told Melanie and after finishing their meal, they skipped coffee and found Dan and Nayna waiting for them in the now busy bar.

They caught up on events and Patrick was delighted to learn that Dan was not only now a DI but was based in North Yorkshire Police HQ at Newby Wiske Hall, near Northallerton, just eighteen miles across the moors from Abbot's Meadow.

Agreeing to meet up soon, Patrick and Melanie set off for home under a bright full moon, Patrick thinking just what a strange quirk of fate it was meeting Dan again, but his thoughts soon strayed to Melanie as she relaxed in the passenger seat, eyes closed and breathing quietly, looking a picture of contentment.

The house was quite cold when they returned as Patrick had forgotten to set the oil fired central heating and the log burner had almost gone out.

He tried to stir the flames up and put a few more logs on, which soon sparked into life, casting a warm glow across the room where they enjoyed sharing the rich and smooth amber flavours of an expensive bottle of Hennessey X.O., a book launch present from Giles, who he was sure would be hounding him sometime very soon.

"Nayna seems very nice" beamed a glowing Melanie "I can't believe she has two children, she looks so tiny"
"Not getting broody?"
"No, but .... " letting the pause lengthen whilst looking into his eyes.
Wondering if she was serious or just a little tipsy, she had been drinking Bellini and most of the bottle of wine as well as the brandy, Patrick broke the spell "Yes, they seem very happy together, I was very friendly with Dan when we were in the Met, he was always one of the good guys, did everything by the book and always had your back, it was good to see him again. Nice for us to have friends over here as well as Cheshire", thinking that they had a few individual and joint friends over in Manchester and Cheshire, which they would still keep in touch with as Melanie would be over there all week, but nice to have an old friend here.

The coffee maker had bestowed a lovely aroma in the room and he poured two steaming mugs at Melanie's insistence, doubting though whether this would affect her sleep as her intense blue eyes were already beginning to droop as she curled up on the sofa in front of the now roaring fire.

She put her mug on the side table and was soon sleeping, giving Patrick time to think about all the possibilities. Was it drugs? Was Novotny the main man? Why had he disappeared so quickly? Where had he gone to?

Soon he would need to find answers to these questions and fortunately, he now had Dan to help, but for now he lifted his own sleeping beauty and carried her upstairs, laid her softly on the bed so as not to wake her and covered her with the duvet.

Patrick lay awake in the dark at 6am on Sunday morning next to Melanie who didn't appear to have moved all night. He would need to ensure that she left for home mid-afternoon so that she could drive home in the light as it was dark now before 7pm and next weekend saw the end of British Summertime and the start of the long dark nights heralding winter with it's cold, frosty mornings and here on the Moors the frequent snowfalls where nothing moved for days at a time.

Still, that was later, he still had the rest of the day with Melanie to look forward to and a drive around the area taking in the scenery followed by lunch at The Red Lion seemed a plan, particularly as this would afford him the opportunity to have a surreptitious look at the proposed drop site, although what he was supposed to drop he still had no idea, but he reached the conclusion that the only way to find out was to ask.

Melanie came down stairs after 9am, showered and dressed in jeans and a soft pink cashmere crew neck sweater, Patrick's socks and smelling like freshly picked freesias.

The aroma of freshly brewed coffee and bacon slowly frying on the AGA filled the kitchen and as this was a Sunday morning, the melodious bells chiming in the crenelated tower of the small 16th-century village church of St. Peter's over a mile and a half away on the other side of Abbot's Meadow could be clearly heard.

"It'll seem very quiet next week when you've gone home".
"You'll still have Mrs. Weston", Melanie joked.
"That's true and at least if you're not here I may even get some writing done before Giles calls".
"I promise I'll call every day", she committed to a delighted Patrick as this was something that she had never done before and despite how close they were, they could sometimes go five or six days without calling, particularly before he left the police force. He hoped this was a sign that she had enjoyed the weekend as much as he had and a sign that maybe they were getting closer than ever. What did they say about absence making the heart grow fonder?

Sunday Lunch in The Red Lion was better than hoped for as instead of the stereotypical steak and chips, fish and chips, gammon and chips etc., they were greeted by a well laid out Carvery table with a choice of roast beef, roast turkey, and local gammon, all looking very appetising with a large selection of fresh vegetables and at a very reasonable price.

He checked himself thinking that he could now afford almost whatever he wanted for lunch whenever he wanted it, or maybe he was adopting the well-versed opinion of Yorkshireman being extremely tight, agreed by everyone that is, except a Yorkshireman.

As Melanie packed her Antler weekender bag, Patrick genuinely didn't want her to go but whilst he knew that she had to be at work Monday and he had tonight's operation to plan, he couldn't resist playfully inviting back to bed for an hour, an invitation she readily accepted.

Waving her off at the gates, Patrick for the first time felt mixed emotions, sad that she was going, full of the joys of a wonderful weekend and excited about her visit next weekend and was already beginning to make plans for this.

Back inside he quickly donned his wax jacket, which still had a lingering smell of Melanie's perfume as they had hung together on the kitchen door, and Timberland boots and set off for the village green to reconnoiter tonight's drop site. Hopefully when he saw the site he would be able to devise some kind of plan and begin to make sense of all the strange events.

Deciding to conceal himself in the shrubbery of a large house opposite the Village Green, which he later found out belonged to local Conservative MP Ian Townsend, which had a clear view of the black, wrought iron, council waste bin, he went home to prepare.

Wearing all black clothing and an old black, woolly hat, Patrick settled down between two Rhododendron bushes behind the garden's dry-stone wall adjacent to the footpath and waited at 8.00pm.

Being this early he thought that he would be able to see any activity around the Green as well as anyone trying to hide in gardens, just as he was, or any parked vehicles.

8.30pm came and went with the village still seemingly asleep with even the pubs appearing deserted.

By 10.00pm Patrick decided that no one was coming and remaining in shadows whenever possible made his way home wondering why go to the trouble and take the risk of arranging a drop-off and not turning up?

Walking through the gates of Oaktree Farm on his return gave him the answer as the front door was open and the window to his lounge on the side of the building had been smashed.

The alarm box had been sprayed with foam insulation to hide the flashing light and kill the noise.

The kitchen had been unceremoniously searched with all the drawers open and Patrick's instinct was to check the office.

Although there were dirty footprints on the stairs and carpet, it seemed that his intruders had been unable to break-in, taking out their frustration on the bedroom by emptying all the drawers and wardrobes onto the floor.

Whatever it was they were looking for they clearly hadn't found it.

There was no real damage or loss, so he set about clearing the mess, Mrs. Weston would be in tomorrow to sort out what he didn't finish tonight.

When Mrs. Weston had finished, and left on Monday lunchtime the house was clean and tidy and smelled like a hospital, all his clothes were back in the proper drawer or wardrobe, the broken window had been repaired by the local handyman and the sun had begun to shine. It felt like home again.

Chapter 10

Wolverhampton All-Weather track tried to make the best of the crisp, chill end of Autumn before the desolate, dark, icy days of Winter set in, when people wanted to stay indoors by the fireside and watch their sport on TV from the comfort of their armchairs.

Six of Mullins transporters were booked out and Adams had three runners to carry down to Wolverhampton.
With six transporters working, Adams knew that Mullins would be driving one of them and thoughtfully gave Mullins a couple of "Banker Bets" at the Midlands Course, certain that he would be unable to resist the opportunity to raid the bookmakers again.

"Monday, same place, two-thirty?"
"OK".

The assignation was made and Adams was almost bursting with impatience as he pictured Stella's naked body.

The transporter collected the three horses from Monk's Lane Stables at six-thirty on Monday morning and Adams was relieved to see it was Mullings driving.

"Dovecote and Aniseed Ball is it then Michael?"

"Yes and you may want a little each-way bet on Mister Softee in the big handicap, he has a chance at the weights and he'll be a good price, should be at least 20/1".

"Right you are then, see you tonight".

"Good luck".

"What's luck got to do with it?" laughed Mullins who was now feeling invincible with his quality information and occasional "Luck of the Irish" as he hauled up the ramp and fastened it securely with the locking bolts.

Adams was there at two o'clock, waiting impatiently, not just because he wanted to get into bed with Stella, though he knew already that would be another magical hour or so, but because he had thought about her more every day and had to try to do something about it.

What was the famous quotation, "Faint Heart never won Fair Lady?"

He had conveniently buried in the back of his mind the dalliance he had seen between Stella and Bălan and had convinced himself that it must have been Bălan trying it on with her, definitely not the other way around. After all, it was only twenty-four hours after she had given herself to him at The Grouse and her body told him then that it was not simply "a bit of fun", even if she *was* reluctant to admit it.

She was late, what could have gone wrong? Mullins was on his way to Wolverhampton, he knew that she had understood the message, so where could she be?

He was as impatient as a schoolboy on a promise and was stupidly on the point of calling her mobile when the black Mercedes pulled into the car park and parked up next to him.

He calmed down, "take a deep breath" he told himself as Stella got out of her car and smiled at him, blipping her remote central locking and walking around the front when he saw that she was wearing a black mini-skirt and a white vest top under an open black jacket, with it appeared from experience, nothing else underneath.
Adams could scarcely control himself and after kissing her almost pushed her into the pub where Coral already had the key to Room 3 waiting on the bar.
Following her upstairs, the view from behind was pure erotica and he fumbled with the key as the thrill of what was to follow made him shake with anticipation.

They made love, or more correctly devoured each other noisily and energetically with a passion that he had not felt for a very long time, and lay panting, their hot, sweaty bodies next to each other as they kissed.

Then came his first mistake, "I want us to be together", he boldly announced to an unsuspecting Stella.
"What?"
"I want us to...".
"I know what you said, I mean what do you mean, you want us to be together?"

"You knew from the start that there were no strings, it's impossible", she continued, her mind began to race, was this the end of the fun and the start of trouble?

"It's not impossible Stella, I love you".

"Oh, no, no, no, no!" she cried, as she made for the black and white tiled En-suite and slammed the door behind, sliding the bolt as she entered.

Adams heard the rushing water of the shower as he sat on the edge of the bed, not understanding her reaction, surely she could not have done the things she had done with him and to him over the past few months and not wanted more, it was inconceivable that she would want to stay at home with Mullins when they could have this all every night.

He was confused.

He was not only confused when she emerged from the shower, but angry.

"Will he still want you when he knows that we've been sleeping together at every opportunity?" he threatened, when she turned on him and grabbed him by the throat, "Don't ever threaten me, no one threatens me, understand? Do you understand?", she had a wild look in her eyes that was so far removed from the person he had just made love to as to have been an entirely different person. "I'm going, and don't ever call me again and if you want to make trouble think again, it may be the last thing you ever do!"

With that she ran from the room, leaving him shocked and sitting naked on the bed with red finger-marks each side of his throat which would develop into bruises, wondering just how he could have been so wrong.

Or perhaps it was just that he had not prepared her for the idea? Perhaps she just needed a bit of time to get used to it?"

That was mistake number two.

Chapter 11

The pink fluorescent "Veronicas" sign flickered like a silent cry for help in the cool, wet October evening outside "Veronica's" Adults Only Club in John Street, just off the redeveloping Attercliffe Road in Sheffield, the blink of the sign reflecting off the bald heads of the two heavily built doormen like two Belisha Beacons at each end of a pedestrian crossing.

The electric blue and pink neon sign announcing "Live Girls & Massage" flashing on and off, deliberately this time, in the blanked-out windows acted as a solicitous magnet for businessmen and visiting clients finishing work before heading for the congested M1 motorway, which would not clear until at least 7 o'clock, even later should there be the usual accident in the ever-present road works. It was a common misconception that Motorways in Britain were built to reduce journey times.

Inside, the loud, hypnotic music invited the early evening customers to engage young girls, scantily dressed in little more than G-strings, suspender belts and matching stockings and only occasional bra, in performing expensive, exotic dances and even more expensive "other services", which depending on the girl and the depth of the clients wallets knew few boundaries, but only after drinking the obligatory, extortionately priced champagne served at shadowy tables by stiletto-heeled, mini-skirted waitress with mobile card terminals attached to broad belts..

The girls, either Eastern European or Thai, with local girls usually only employed behind the bar or in the dimly lit cloakroom, were confirmed by a dog-eared A4 laminated sheet in the entrance as all being "over 18", satisfying the local licensing authority, but to any outsider, some girls, particularly the Asians, looked no older than early teens at best. The Police regularly visited to inspect the girl's passports and the club membership lists to satisfy the legal requirements had been met but the management always had at least 24 hours' notice of any inspection, either formally or by way of a friendly phone call, as no one wanted the embarrassment of being flagged as frequenters of the premises, regardless of their rank.

The forced smiles of the girls gave the illusion of having a good time and satisfied most of the clients, those clients who were not could take up any complaint with Customer Services, in the form of the unforgiving doormen. After all, who was going to complain, particularly as three-quarters of the clients were either high-profile figures or married men, or both.

The doormen usually worked in pairs and knew all the regulars, some visiting almost every night like clockwork and usually demanding the services of the same girl, in some ways the routine differed little to being married, except that the girls were keen, never had headaches and for a price would do most things that wives would never do.

As well as keeping out troublemakers, of which there were few, the doormen also took responsibility for ensuring the girls did as they were told and any who thought they could walk away from their employment soon found out differently. The doormen usually relied on the threats to the girls or their families in their homeland but nevertheless were skilled at leaving no marks, should this amount of persuasion be necessary, as the punters were less keen on girls looking like they had been in a nasty accident and besides, the loss of income from girls who were unable to work also meant their usefulness would be questionable.

Girls who were trouble causers didn't last long at Veronica's and were often not seen or heard from again, their fate being speculated on by the other girls which tended to keep them in line. They understood they were captive but the repercussions to them and their families were fearsome enough to be an effective deterrent to escaping and the majority of the girls were simply resigned to their lives, many desperate enough to rely on drugs which were supplied to ensure both reliance on their captors and as a mental barrier to the iniquitous lifestyle they were forced to endure.

Over the past two years three girls had disappeared.

Angela and Suzanne, Eastern Europeans, had tried to simply walk out one Thursday evening and hitch lifts to wherever they could, but both were picked up before reaching the motorway and simply disappeared.

Chloe, the tall 19-year-old Rumanian girl with long, flowing dark-brown curls, dark brown eyes and a Playboy Centrefold body, was a lot smarter than the others and sought to secure the approval of a man who had become a regular on Tuesday and Friday nights, the main attraction being she had discovered that he was a journalist.

Seeing the opportunity to use him as a means of blackmail she believed she had only to give him the full story about the use of the girls as sex slaves to force them to let her walk away and so for three months she made him feel "special" and made sure that he never asked for anyone else, teasing him about her usefulness as an informer and her willingness to give him a big story, one that could make his reputation as a journalist.

The merciless reach and resourcefulness of the Rumanian Mafia owners, however, ensured that as Chloe and her client became close, they made sure they knew all about Mr. Jonathan Price of the Sheffield Star who had previously written two exposés which made the Nationals.

On a dry and windy night in early November, he bought a drink at the bar and scanned the floor for the beautiful Chloe.
Quieter than most Thursday evenings at this time, possibly because of the realisation that Christmas and all the associated expense was just seven weeks away, the more muscular of the two doormen on duty took a stool next to him.

Without blinking he looked him in the eye, asking him how Dawn his wife and two small children, Jamie 4 and Jessica 2 were and verifying that the new double glazing at 22 Lime Tree Close in Chesterfield must have cost a few grand.

He was told that they loved children and had never hurt one, but of course, there was always a first time for everything. He agreed with the doorman's suggestion that it would be advisable not to go to the club again or speak to anyone about the conversation; this meant Chloe, his editor, the police, anyone.

Just to be sure he was escorted by the elbow in a vice-like grip to the Gents toilet where he was professionally searched by the two doormen on duty to ensure he had no recording devices and his iPhone was destroyed by a steel-tipped heel, before punches to the kidneys dropped him to his knees which left him in no doubt of the reality of their threats. "I'm sure we understand each other, yes?" said the heavily accented doorman and without waiting left the toilets to allow Jonathan to slowly attempt to stand without collapsing before walking slowly and deliberately across the club.

"Goodnight Sir", meeting with the menacing eyes of the kidney specialist, "Hope not to see you again", was said with a smile as Jonathan half walked, half staggered from the club into the cold, dark evening which had suddenly become much less pleasant.

Jonathan was not prepared to risk the safety of his family however much he wanted to protect Chloe and the others or indeed to sell the story to the nationals.

He knew that despite his indiscretions he loved his wife and realised that he had to simply walk away and turn a blind eye to the situation feeling that if he did so, they would be safe, as he already had the information he needed to make big trouble for the owners of Veronicas and if his family was hurt, he would not hesitate to use it with the London papers and Police just a call away.

If, however, he had wanted to be a martyr and help, there was still the pain in his back from his bruised kidneys to remind him of the consequences of any ill-advised acts of bravery.

Chapter 12

Patrick's neighbours moving eastwards away from Abbot's Meadow, albeit over a mile away, were John and Charlotte Darby at Margrave Stables.
Patrick loved being back in Yorkshire so much that he was beginning to think that he may well put down roots here and with that in mind he thought it time to introduce himself to his neighbours.

John and Charlotte had taken over the stables from Charlotte's father, Cyril Watkins, who had trained at Margrave for 40 years before retiring, at which point he received an MBE for his services to racing.

He had trained over 5000 winners and had twice been champion trainer, no small feat for a northern based yard and whilst he had trained a 2000gns winners, two 1000gns winners, an Oaks winner and a St. Leger winner, The Derby had eluded him, although he had twice trained runners-up, one of which Ebony Keys, was deemed to have been a very unlucky second when a tired pacemaker pushed him very wide around Tattenham Corner and it took his jockey over a furlong to make up the ground and hit the front half a furlong from home but just ran out of legs and was beaten by a head by the fast finishing Godolphin favourite, Captain Cook.

John was a 50-year-old, typical trainer, from the brown felt trilby to the belted Macintosh, who had lived and breathed horses all his life. His father had been a trainer in East Illesley close to Newbury and when he died left the reigns to his elder son Nigel in his will, much to the chagrin of John.

John had however met Cyril's daughter Charlotte at the Doncaster St. Leger meeting a year previously and the attraction was instantaneous.

He had never seen such a striking girl in his life. Long flowing auburn hair, emerald green eyes, and freckles. Why he found freckles so irresistible he didn't know but remembered a girl called Susan at junior school who was his first real love and she sported freckles although having long dark hair. Everyone said that Charlotte took after her mother Carole for looks, which she was very pleased about as her mother had died from breast cancer when she was just 6 years old and her memories of her mother were fading no matter how much she tried to keep them alive and she sometimes wondered just how much was real and how much was imagined emotions.

Fortunately, Charlotte was also attracted to John in much the same way and they spent the afternoon sipping champagne whilst watching her father's Classic hope St. Petersburg finish an impressive third of fifteen runners despite not liking the going and just failing to get up, finished beaten by just two lengths.

Both wanted to see each other again as soon possible but were reluctant to make the suggestion first for fear of being rejected and as often happens, they started to speak at the same time, looking into each other's eyes and bursting into a fit of laughter when they knew just what the other was about to say.

Afterwards, they spent as much time as possible with each other and were very much in love. Cyril thought he was a good judge of people as well as horses and seeing his daughter so happy and knowing all about the situation with Nigel, asked John to move into the gatehouse, a small, stone built, 2-bedroom house just inside the old gated entrance at the end of the driveway to the stables, which John happily agreed to do.

He moved to Abbot's Meadow in a snowy January to help get the string up to speed for the new turf season in March and he and Charlotte had scarcely been apart since.

Cyril and John worked well together and the 40-strong yard that season produced 189 winners and amassed just under £2 million in prize money.

Cyril's health, however, suffered a severe setback when he was diagnosed with prostate cancer in August and John carried the yard for the rest of the season much to the delight of the loyal owners who were concerned that their assets would deteriorate with the incapacity of Cyril and were ready to move their horses to other yards should this be the case. However, it was very much business as usual and the impressive results, particularly with some of the stables less talented horses, ensured that no owners left and indeed the biggest two patrons, Sir John Whitfield and Lady Marlborough, assured Cyril that they intended to purchase a few 2-year-olds for the following season and wanted to send them to Margrave even if Cyril was unable to carry on, if John oversaw them.

This was extremely good news for Cyril on several fronts. He could retire, happily knowing that the business was in good hands, his loyal owners who had become friends over many years would remain with Margrave and he was sure that Charlotte's relationship with John would continue to flourish and that she would have a secure future, both emotionally and financially.

John was proud to accept Cyril's proposal of taking on the yard and a few days later Charlotte was delighted to accept John's somewhat clumsy proposal they should get married as he was going to take over the yard.

Luckily she knew John so well that whilst he made it sound like a business proposal, she had always known from their first meeting at Doncaster that someday they would be married, so had no hesitation in accepting.

Interestingly, brother Nigel's fortunes were less than glamorous, with the yard steadily declining and Nigel seemingly unable or unwilling to take any action to build upon his legacy.

John and Charlotte were married in a small ceremony in early December in the 16th century St. Peter's Church in the heart of Abbot's Meadow after which Cyril insisted that they moved into the main Lodge whilst he moved into the Gatehouse, giving them space to hopefully raise a family.

Cyril had never remarried and doted on Charlotte and the thought of one day having grandchildren was his final dream particularly as he and Carole would have liked a bigger family and had made such great plans until her illness and eventual death had meant that this would never be possible. Cyril still missed her and thought of her every day and felt her presence in and around the stables and so couldn't bear to consider ever moving away from the home they shared together which until John's arrival was a fear he had always had at the back of his mind. Charlotte was a constant reminder of his beloved Carole, who had grown to resemble her mother in so many ways, he could see her mother every time she smiled, which was almost all of the time, particularly since she had met John and now she had come through the typical rebellious teenage years which Cyril had to confess he had found so difficult raising her on his own, but he was rightly proud of the end result for Charlotte had grown into not only a beautiful woman, but one with a great knowledge of racing and a good head for business, a rare commodity and a partner for John in more ways than one.

Patrick decided that the brisk walk to Margrave stables on this calm, cool, cloudless autumn evening would be good for him and only when he had set off had he realised just how dark the countryside could be. Without the benefit of street lighting and no torch, the lack of "light pollution" meant that the stars were brighter than he ever imagined and this combined with the quiet of the night, with no traffic noise from any nearby major roads, gave the place an almost surreal feel.

Eventually, having strained his eyes at times to see by starlight the verges on the roadside in an effort to keep on the road, he came to the gatehouse, with just a single window lit up, and made out the driveway to the stables with the impressive double-fronted stone built lodge standing illuminated by two tasteful Victorian lamp posts.

Having earlier telephoned to say he would like to call and introduce himself this evening, his knock on the dark green, solid oak front door was answered almost immediately by John, casually dressed in brown corduroy trousers, open-necked checked twill shirt and heavy beige cardigan with leather elbow patches, obviously sewn on later, and leather buttons, looking anything but the successful trainer he had expected.

"Come in, you must be Patrick".

"Thank you and you must be John", Patrick replied to the warm greeting, the smell of baking bread and the welcoming aroma of freshly brewed coffee spilling out into the doorway.

Charlotte appeared in the kitchen doorway on the right, at the end of the long parquet floored hallway, looking the part of homemaker, with a Crabtree & Evelyn logoed apron and oven gloves.
Before John could introduce her, she called out with a wide smile,
"Come on in Patrick, I'm Charlotte, but everyone calls me Charlie. Hope you're hungry, supper will be ready in half an hour".

Although Patrick had not expected a meal the aroma of home cooking intensified a growing hunger.

"Come into the lounge and make yourself comfortable, drink? wine? scotch?", asked John leading the way off to the first doorway on the left.

"Whatever you're having is fine, thank you".

Charlie, devoid of the apron, joined them wearing tight denim jeans and a russet coloured cashmere roll-necked sweater that showed off all her considerable assets and perfectly complemented her striking long, auburn wavy hair and beguiling freckles. "Pour me a large sherry darling", she said to John who was busily pouring three fingers of Glenmorangie into each of two beautifully cut Waterford lead crystal whisky glasses before he retrieved a similarly cut schooner from the dark oak dresser for Charlie's pale Tio Pepe.

"So how are you finding Abbot's Meadow?" inquired John when they were all seated on the well-used but extremely comfortable burgundy brocade upholstered Steed suite, John and Charlie on the large three-seater whilst Patrick settled himself into the armchair next to the wood burning stove, seemingly the heating of choice in these parts.

"It's a bit like coming home", replied Patrick, "I was born in Yorkshire but moved away when I was small and I have rarely been back unless it's been on a case".

"A case? We had heard you were a writer", chipped in Charlie.

"Only recently, before that I was in the Met and Greater Manchester Police on the Serious Crime squads but I decided when the opportunity came up that it was time do something different and my publisher thought that I could make a career from writing. Trying to find the peace and quiet to write however was very difficult in Manchester as even when I was not working there was always some friend bobbing in for a coffee or wanting to take me somewhere for a drink or a meal, so I decided to move here and I can't believe just how peaceful it is".

"It may seem peaceful but you know what they say about villages being hotbeds of sin, there are a lot of things happening here that beg questions. Take your farm for instance; Who was the last owner? Where did he come from? What was he doing? Where did he go? The village is rife with rumour and speculation, but then that's just typical of a village".

Charlie went to check on supper as he confided in John.

"It's interesting that you say that because there are a few things that have happened that don't make any sense, such as someone stealing his belongings that he left in one of the stables, and brazenly at that", but before he received any further comment or questions a welcomed, "right I think supper's ready boys", called them through to the kitchen.

He was pleased that the evening wasn't too formal and the large, well-used, solid oak refectory table was laid only at one end with Charlie at the head and Patrick and John at either side.

"Something smells good", he said sincerely as the delicious smells emanating from the AGA promised much.

"Just a casserole", replied Charlie modestly, as she was a great cook and as she regularly cooked for all the stable hands who lived in as well as John and her father, she had plenty of practice.

The chicken in red wine with Dijon mustard dumplings and chive mashed potatoes was delicately flavoured with just a hint of garlic and tarragon and was simply delicious.

"You certainly know how to cook", complimented Patrick appreciatively.

"I know my place", Charlie replied tongue-in-cheek and helped herself to another glass of 2010 Clotte Saint Emilio, a very smooth and expensive Bordeaux. They were certainly not short of a few pounds Patrick thought if they could be drinking this quality of wine for a midweek supper, even if they were trying to impress a guest, which they didn't appear to be, being very relaxed and comfortable and this was turning into a very nice evening.

With his training and background, he believed himself to be a good judge of people and he found he was very easy with his new neighbours, deciding he would return the invitation when Melanie next visited and was sure that Charlie and Melanie would get on well as they also shared a passion for horses.

The evening progressed through a delicious home-made Tiramisu, how could she know it was one of his favourite treats from childhood Christmases and evoked pleasant memories, to a superb cheeseboard and aged Port and finishing with a very smooth Courvoisier 12-Year-Old Connoisseur Collection Cognac, he would see what John thought of his Hennessey when they came to him.

The conversations were light and friendly and never stilted, asking each other about interests, backgrounds, and life in general until the kitchen clock chimed eleven.

Knowing that the first string would be out on the gallops at seven in the morning, Patrick decided to take his leave.

He declined the offer of a lift home, they had both drunk well over the limit, and knew he would enjoy the walk home, full of the warm glow of the alcohol and the superb supper but pleased he had decided to wear his overcoat.
The first vestige of an evening frost under the ebony, cloudless sky promised a cold night to come, the grass verges crunching under his feet as he frequently strayed from the roadway in the pitch-black evening.

He heard the vehicle approaching a good way off on such a still night but it was upon him very quickly and fortunately as he was facing the oncoming traffic he was able to jump into the hedge over the ditch as the 4x4 drove straight at him and then sped away before he could see the number plates.

Was it deliberate or just that the driver didn't see him without the benefit of street lighting?

Chapter 13

The wind had increased dramatically in the last couple of hours, whipping across Underbank Reservoir to the north of Sheffield and on the edge of the bleak and exposed Peak District National Park, creating foot-high, white-topped waves that rocked the boat in which Stephen and his son Max were fishing for Pike.

The autumn light was failing fast and Stephen decided that enough was enough and started the small outboard motor to set off for home, looking forward to a warm mug of Tomato soup in front of the open fire in their chalet style, semi-detached in Ecclesfield, 10 miles away.

They had caught two Pike, one "Jack Pike" a little over 7lbs. and a better one of 14lbs 12oz as their scales informed them, not bad for four hours fishing and at just £3 for a day ticket was not an expensive day. Being a true Yorkshireman, this was of great importance.

Typically, as soon as he had reeled in his almost fluorescent blue and yellow spinner bait to start the engine, Max had a bite. "Dad, this feels like a whopper", shouted an excited Max, shouting being the operative word as the sound of the wind was becoming louder by the minute.

"Just wind it in, if your line breaks it breaks, let's just get off home", stammered a Dad increasingly concerned about the conditions.

"Dad, what is it?" asked Max as a dark, heavy mass surfaced some thirty feet away in the dusky light.

Peering intently at the shape, he saw clothing and ropes; "Cut your line", yelled a frightened Stephen, realising that this was something that a boy of ten shouldn't see.

Snatching the rod from a curious Max, who still had not realised what was happening, Stephen cut the line himself and turning the boat away from the bound body, headed to the reservoir bank with the wind behind them as fast as they could go.

Crashing the boat up the shingle banking, physically hoisting Max onto shore, dragging the boat out of the water and scrambling up the banking to the shelter of the overhanging trees, much to the annoyance of a gaggle of Canada Geese who let their displeasure be known before taking to the air towards the north end of the body of water with the Pennines now just a dark shadow on the skyline, Stephen felt his legs beginning to shake, so much in fact that he was unable to stand and crashed to the wet banking where he sat recovering his composure for what seemed forever, although actually just a few minutes.

A subdued and white Max began to shiver with cold and Stephen judged correctly, in shock, he carried his son bodily to the car just 50 metres away where, having seated him in the security of the passenger seat, he turned on the engine and heater, retrieved his phone and closing the car door behind him dialed 999 with still trembling, white fingers.

"Police, Ambulance or Fire" inquired the calming, firm voice of the operator.

"Police" answered Stephen with more authority in his voice than he felt.

Just thirteen minutes later, sitting in the car with a now warm Max who was still very quiet but had at least stopped shaking, he heard the first of a succession of sirens screaming along the A616 Stocksbridge by-pass.

The two officers in the first car began to question Stephen as to what he had seen as an empathetic ambulance crew attended to Max, wrapping him in what looked to be a roll of tin foil and checking all his signs, understanding how shock can affect people of all ages.

"We're going to need divers and CSI Sarge" insisted the authoritative, bubbly blonde WPC Maggie Bell, "there's a body, apparently tied up about 100 metres from the bank"

"Stay there, secure the scene and keep everyone away, I'll get a team out there as soon as poss."

Disliking Sgt Philips intensely as he frequently made unwelcome passes at her, Maggie wondered just how many people would be contaminating a crime scene a hundred yards out in a dark, bitterly cold, windswept reservoir.

However, she knew that the body was dumped into the water from somewhere on the three miles plus perimeter and wherever it entered could provide vital clues, but two PC's to protect the site integrity of three miles of banking? "in your dreams Sarge!" she mumbled to herself.

After Stephen and Max had been given the OK by the ambulance crew and given their version of events to the more experienced and calming PC Williams, they were allowed home with a promise of a visit by a PC in the next twenty-four hours to take formal statements.

The Yorkshire and the Humber Underwater Search & Marine Unit in the form of a Sergeant and two trained constables arrived ninety minutes later from their base in Humberside, towing their rigid inflatable boat, complete with sonar behind the brightly liveried Mitsubishi L200 and entered via the Stocksbridge Sailing Club entrance, just 400 metres from where the submerged "body" had been encountered.

Experience told them that until they had located the object, they would reserve judgement on whether it was, in fact, a body.

However, the alleged body had disappeared again and it was imperative that it was located and brought ashore as quickly as possible to preserve any possible forensic evidence, always assuming it was (a) a body and (b) that there was any evidence to find.

By the time the search divers were ready to start their search, three additional PC's and a DS had arrived on the scene followed by two CSIs based in Carbrook in Sheffield hoping that this was indeed a suicide as anything more complicated threatened to eat into their planned weekends, although if the witnesses were to be believed, suicides didn't usually manage to tie themselves up first.

WPC Bell and her colleague PC Jason Williams had already found what seemed to be the entry site 200 metres north of the Sailing Club and there was now a taped cordon around the area, despite the howling wind and the steadily increasing rain doing their best to obliterate any potential clues left for CSI to identify.

The currents on the reservoir were notoriously unreliable and could have taken the "body" some distance from the original location. Given that the autumn dusk had turned into a dark, moonless night, Sergeant Michael Judge in charge of the search team contacted his boss Inspector Armitage and agreed that they would begin their search at first light, conditions permitting.

Sgt Philips seemed to take great delight in leaving Bell and Williams to safeguard the windswept, inhospitable site, until their replacements came on shift and made their way there by 11pm, some four hours later.

The search team was joined on site at 7.30am the following morning by the CSI team when, fortunately, the wind had abated and the day had started bright, dry and particularly mild for October. As light broke, an object could be seen floating two hundred metres out from the dam wall and the officers retrieved the body and brought it ashore in a matter of minutes.

Immediately the object was confirmed to be a body and the circumstances suspicious, especially as it was bound with blue nylon rope and had a hole in the forehead, the highly experienced 60-year-old South Yorkshire Police Pathologist, Welshman Dr. Mervyn Lewis was called to the scene together with the 35 years old Oxbridge fast-tracked, tall, athletic, black Detective Inspector Courtney Bradshaw, meeting on site with a cacophony of sirens.

"Well, Dr. Lewis?" asked an impatient DI Bradshaw. "Well, DI Bradshaw, unless the victim somehow learned the trick of tying himself up and adding weights to his feet before shooting himself in the head and then throwing himself in the reservoir, I'd say it wasn't suicide", replied Dr. Lewis with more than a hint of sarcasm, particularly as he had missed his customary Saturday morning round of golf at nearby Wortley Golf Club and now looked destined to spend the day with Mrs. Lewis who he was convinced was a professional clothes shopper.

"How long ago?", replied DI Bradshaw

"Hard to say, but my first guess, I stress guess mind, would be that looking at the level of decomposition, he has been in the water for 2 to 3 weeks but I'll tell you more after the PM which fortunately I can do as a priority on Monday morning".

Some priority, 2 days for a murder victim while the team would be forced to spend the weekend guessing who, where, why and how with very little evidence to go on other than fingerprints, "See if he's on the system James?" she asked DS Wakefield impatiently.

"Any chance you could take a look at him any sooner Doc?"

"You're lucky I'm not too busy at the moment, it'll be Monday morning 8.00am, I'll see you there", he shouted over his shoulder, walking away to the car, his mind firmly fixed on whether he might still fit in 9-holes.

"Wouldn't miss it for the world!" said a very irritated Bradshaw.

The CSI team got to work on the entry site and although very little evidence was likely to be found given the time period and the weather, they spent the whole of Saturday going over every stone and blade of grass and bagging several items for closer examination at the lab.

Monday morning came with DI Bradshaw still no nearer to finding the identity of the body as the fingerprint search came back with no matches and she just hoped that Dr. Lewis could provide some clues. She walked into the mortuary sucking on two extra strong mints and had a reserve supply stashed inside her charcoal leather blouson should she need them. She didn't think that she would ever get used to the putrid smell of rotting flesh and believed that this morning would be particularly unpleasant.

DS James Wakefield and DC Vicky Stanhope, part of the CID team, were already outside waiting as DI Bradshaw got out of her new, sleek black 3-series BMW.
"Good morning boss," they said in unison.
"Let's hope so, the sooner we can start on this enquiry the better, we've already wasted 2 days as some people are on a cushy number", she replied and walked through the door held open by DS Wakefield.

Suitably clothed in green overalls and white rubber boots, Dr. Lewis entered the theatre and wished a good morning to his two assistants who DI Bradshaw knew from previous PMs.
Looking at the police presence he mumbled,

"Good morning all, hope you had a good weekend? Let's get started, shall we?", and turning on the tape recorder to record all of his observations he started to cut off the man's clothes.

The smell emanating from the three-week-old corpse was sickening but when Lewis turned on the circular saw having peeled back the victim's scalp and proceeded to remove the top of the man's skull, DC Stanhope paled to a deathly white and was escorted quickly out of the room by an attentive DS Wakefield before she threw up into a waste bin by the front door just as she made it into the fresh air.

DI Bradshaw showed no emotion, remembering her first time and looking at the chuckling Pathologist thought how grateful she was to have a "real job" that didn't involve dissecting people who had denaturised into rotten meat five days a week.

Still, at least it *was* only five days, unlike CID.

DS Wakefield entered the room a few minutes later and nodded to Bradshaw to confirm that Vicky was OK, how sweet!

A somewhat embarrassed DC Stanhope re-entered the theatre a while later just as Dr. Lewis was summarising; "A male, 45 to 50 years old, probably Mid-European judging by the dentistry, died approximately 18 to 20 days ago, sorry I can't be more specific because of the time in the water.

Signs of being beaten extensively with a thick bar, possibly a baseball bat or similar, as evidenced with the broken left arm and extensive bruising to back, head and legs, before being shot at point-blank range in the forehead.

Attacker probably right handed not sure that that will help much. The bullet is a .22 calibre which lodged itself in the rear of the brain, I've recovered this for ballistics. Also, a broken leg in childhood around the age of 8. You'll have my full report by tomorrow afternoon"

With that, Lewis hurried out of the room leaving his assistants to clean up ready for the next corpse.

"What a job eh", thought Bradshaw planning their next actions.

Back outside she asked, "OK Vicky?"

"Yeah, sorry boss".

"You'll get used to it, make sure you take plenty of mints in with you next time, it helps," Bradshaw said knowingly.

"So nothing from fingerprints on our database but check with Interpol James, we may get lucky. Vicky, can you check for any other executions with a .22 in the last 12 to 18 months on HOLMES and Interpol databases. We'll meet my office at 1pm for a team briefing."

Chapter 14

Bradshaw was greeted on entering the station by the Desk Sergeant, George Darbyshire, known by everyone as "Peaky", not from his surname but from having spent his early career in Buxton, a Spa town in the High Peak in Derbyshire, Darbyshire was more or less a permanent fixture at Carsbrook and had just two years left before retirement, for which he was ticking off the days.

"Thank goodness you're back, your apprentice has been hopping about with a smile like a Cheshire cat", chuckled Peaky, who was on familiar terms with all the station police staff, unless protocol determined titles and ranks.

"Let's hope he's got some good news for me then Peaky", Bradshaw smiled in reply.

DS Wakefield met her at the door waving aloft a sheet of A4 paper from the office printer.

"Pavel Popescu, spent 3 years in Doftana prison in Romania for embezzlement and currently wanted by the Rumanian Police in connection with drug smuggling and people trafficking and believed to be high up in the Romanian Mafia".

"Well then, actually been doing something productive while I've been out have you James?" she asked somewhat lopsidedly as the right-hand side of her face was still frozen by the dentist's local anesthetic as she had just had 2 fillings, must stop eating cakes and sweets from now on she threatened herself.

"Get Vicky and the rest of the team in my office now, oh and bring coffees, no cakes".

DI Bradshaw's office was unlike most DI's offices, which usually emulated the old newspaper editor's desks from old black and white films.

The desk was tidy, the files she was currently working on were stacked neatly in alphabetical order in piles of no more than five, on the floor behind her polished chrome and black imitation leather swivel chair and two air fresheners sat on the window sill to provide a boost for when the team brought bacon sandwiches from the canteen into her office at the customary morning briefings which could last for an hour on occasions.

There was no hint however of this being over the top, it was just how she liked her office and mirrored how she conducted her operations; neat, organised and controlled.

When reports needed to be written, it was not traumatic as she made a point of writing everything up before the end of each shift so that when her boss, the pedantic DCI Simkins asked for an update, which he tended to do at seemingly the most inopportune moments, (was he trying to catch her out?) it was ready and waiting, ensuring she could still get on with the day's tasks uninterrupted.

She wouldn't have it any other way and tried to instil this modus operandi into her subordinates, however irritating this was for them, as she knew this training and discipline eventually led to more productive and professional colleagues and fewer cock-ups!

"Well at least we now know who he is and where he is but he won't be answering any questions for us will he?" started a somber Bradshaw with a hint of a lisp when the team was assembled. "Question is where's he been, what's he been up to and who caught up with him? It certainly looks like an execution so let's hope it is the Mafia that has found him and it's a one off and not some local war about to take place on our patch. So, see what you can find out, circulate his picture to all forces in a 100-mile radius, I can't see them travelling any further than that to dump him can you?"

"On it, boss", replied an enthusiastic WPC Sammie Lindley, 24 years old and newly recruited to CID. With short dark hair and a slim figure which despite being pretty enough with large, nearly black eyes and perfect straight white teeth, made her look from the back just like a boy. She was even beginning to speak like the others.

"According to the Interpol file, Popescu spent three years in Doftana prison for embezzling over one hundred and fifty thousand pounds from his employers, National Bank of Romania. It's believed that whilst in Doftana he was recruited by the Romanian Mafia to work as an accountant, responsible for looking after and hiding many millions of pounds of their funds worldwide, amassed from protection rackets, drug smuggling, and prostitution", relayed a smug DS Wakefield, "I'll call the police in Bucharest who put out the alert and let them know, if I can find anyone who speaks English".

"It's touch and go whether your language can be described as English never mind any Rumanians," Bradshaw remarked sarcastically referring to Wakefield's thick Yorkshire accent.

"Yeah, yeah, but then we didn't all go to prep school did we", was the retort, giving as good as he got.

"Right, we'll meet back here at 6pm and see what breaks".

Back in the open plan office, Wakefield grabbed a piping hot coffee if you could call the light brownie-grey liquid from the vending machine coffee, and a Kit Kat.

Picking up the phone he called the Rumanian number on the Interpol alert.

"Bună dimineața, Poliția București, Sergeant Vasilev Vorbind", came the voice.

"Do you speak English?" shouted Wakefield, unaware of doing what most English people do when speaking to foreigners, shouting as though it will make the other person suddenly understand what they are saying.

"Da, excuse me yes" replied Sergeant Vasilev, much to the relief of Wakefield, "I studied in England at Liverpool University, Chemistry, my name is Anton".

"Thank heavens for that Anton, I'm Detective Sergeant John Wakefield from South Yorkshire CID in Sheffield, England. We have found the body of Pavel Popescu that you have an enquiry lodged through Interpol, file number RO37248"

"Pavel Popescu, wait while I get the details up. Wow! We have been looking for him for a long time, very bad company he keeps, the body you say, that means he is dead yes?"

"Tied up, beaten and shot in the head. What can you tell me about him, does he have any connection that you know about in the UK?"

"The only report we have had in the last two years is that he was sighted boarding a train for Amsterdam, but that was not confirmed. After that nothing. Do you know how long he has been in the UK?"

"No, we only found the body a few days ago and identified him today, that's why I called to check if there is any connection with the UK, any gangs, associates, etc. If you can check and come back to me on this number, I'll deal just with you Anton if that's OK? and I'll keep you posted on anything we find here"
"Thank you, John, I will talk with my colleagues"

It was also known that the Rumanian Mafia guaranteed their employees were kept in line by way of threats to families and loved ones and the Rumanian Police had also noted that they had tried to find what leverage they had on Popescu, but no more information was recorded on the file.

So how did he end up with a bullet in his brain in a freezing cold reservoir in the north of England?

Circulating his photo resulted in a call from North Yorkshire Police in Malton the next morning.

By a stroke of sheer luck, Alan Jones, a young Police Dog Handler who should have been on leave for 5 days but was called in for duty at the mid-week Leeds United v Millwall game at Elland Road, remembered stopping the man three months ago for allegedly speeding on the Abbot's Meadow to Malton Road. Alleged being the appropriate word as they stopped him for overtaking his Police Peugeot Van which was not equipped with the necessary equipment to prove a speeding offence in court and besides as he was in a hurry to get back to the station as the usual moratorium on overtime was on everyone's mind, he simply did a cursory check, recording the registration number of the VW Golf as YU55AZU which was MOT'd, not notified as stolen, was insured, and the driver had a valid driving licence.
Some of his colleagues he knew would simply have put on the blues and twos as a warning and gone off duty if they were not being paid.

Having checked his notes, however, the licence did not belong to Pavel Popescu but to Miroslav Novotny.

Having now checked the Golf registration number it was confirmed as belonging to a Miroslav Novotny of Oaktree Farm, Abbot's Meadow. The next contact would be a visit to the address on the licence by North Yorkshire Police.

Patrick was pleased to see the dynamic duo of DCs Crowe and Miller crunching the gravel on the way to his door, well, pleased to see Heather Miller anyway.

"Good morning Mr. Spencer, may we come in?" asked the ever-popular Crowe, "we need to speak to you about Mr. Miroslav Novotny."
"You can speak all you like but since I never met him I don't know how I can help you Detective Constable", he replied curtly stressing the Constable rank.
"But you did buy the house from him, Mr. Spencer?"
"Yes a couple of weeks before your first visit about the theft from the stables. Have you caught anyone yet?", asked Patrick looking Crowe straight in the eye but sensing the only discomfort came from his female colleague.
"We're working on a few leads", lied Crowe who had issued the all-important crime number and promptly forgotten about it, until this morning that is.
"Why do you want to talk about Novotny anyway?" inquired an interested Patrick.
"He's been found murdered and dumped in a reservoir in Sheffield, so any help you can give us would be gratefully received?"
"Sorry, but you would be better talking to Mrs. Weston, my housekeeper, she'll be in tomorrow from 9am if you want to speak to her".
"Do you have her home address?"

This time, it was Patrick's turn to be suitably embarrassed as he hadn't asked what her address was, she simply turned up when she was expected.
Must get a grip Patrick he said to himself.
"OK, we'll call tomorrow. Thank you for your help Mr. Spencer", said DC Miller closing her notebook and walking quickly down the driveway.

Patrick had no intention of mentioning the threats to Melanie and himself, if any action was needed, he and Dan would take care of it.

Chapter 15

"Right then, question one, "In which country was Cliff Richard born?" boomed Peter Castle's voice over the far too loud PA system as Thursday's Quiz Night started in The Margrave.
The quiz was in four parts, the first three parts consisting of six questions each being chosen from a variety of subjects with the final round a general knowledge round of twelve questions, which came after the supper break.

Quiz Nights were the biggest night of the week for The Margrave with even the village "incomers" venturing out either to try to win the cash prize and roll-over jackpot, or just to sample the delicious home cooked supper of either Chilli con Carne with Jacket Potato or Chicken Curry and Rice which Peter's wife, Lindsay, put on free gratis to encourage customers into the pub, the level of spice and salt ensuring that they also bought plenty of drinks to cover the cost of the food.

After just a few weeks Patrick no longer classed himself as an "Incomer" due to the welcome he had received.
He felt as if he had lived here for years and had almost become one of the locals as he treated everyone the same, whether stable lad, barmaid or trainer just as he had always done wherever he had lived or worked.

He even shared an occasional beer with the remarkably forthright Reverend Gerald Wilson, the 73-year-old vicar of St. Peters, who notoriously ignored anyone who wasn't from the village or didn't attend church, so he considered himself highly honoured.

He found it quite funny however to watch the self-styled middle-classes, who had predominantly moved into the area because of their jobs, forming their own cliques and blatantly ignoring the locals.
Angela had told him on one of his first visits to the Pub that when you moved into the village and joined in you were soon accepted, but keep yourself to yourself and demonstrate any kind of attitude and you would be an Incomer no matter how long you lived in the village and there were times when everyone needed a bit of help.

It was the third Quiz Night in a row that Patrick had attended, and enjoyed the atmosphere and the continual banter from the stable lads and girls from the area's three racing yards, although he didn't enter the quiz as such, feeling that he didn't need the prize money and the questions were pitched below his level of education and experience, he stopped short of the word IQ.

With Christmas, just six weeks away, Lindsay and Angela had already trimmed the 7 feet tall Norwegian Spruce Christmas Tree, the twinkling lights and flickering flames from the log fire producing an almost hypnotic effect.

Patrick felt that with the lighting effects and the background Christmas Carols playing during the interval, he would be sure to look out of the window and see snow falling.

Hopefully, this would be their first Christmas in his new home if Melanie could sort out her schedules with the producers. He felt a tinge of childhood excitement at the thought.

John and Charlie were regulars on Thursdays and since his supper invitation at Margrave Stables, Patrick usually shared a corner table with them near to the Inglenook fireplace where their conversation flowed on any number of topics, usually steering around to racing, horses, Melanie and racing again.

He also found on previous occasions that there was an opportunity to pick up a good tip at the bar for the following weekend's racing, and just last Tuesday he had invested £20 on Short Trigger, which had narrowly won a moderate handicap on the all-weather track at Soutwell at 16/1 after speaking to Justin, who was becoming a real mine of information.

His winnings would certainly stock the freezer from the Black Bull Farm Shop ready for Melanie's next visit which unfortunately would not be until the following weekend, as this weekend she was filling in for Dai Rees on his Sunday Mid-Morning Show, whilst he took a "well earned" break in the sun in Lanzarote.

Justin and a girl called Isla, who was a stranger to Patrick, joined him at the bar as they were the last two stools available in the pub, as he got the drinks in, pints of Black Sheep for him and John and a Dry White Wine for Charlie, and duly asked Justin and Isla if they would like a drink.

Before Justin could accept Isla declined with, "Thanks but we've only just got one".

"Yes, that's OK", stuttered a disappointed Justin as most stable lads never refused the offer of a drink. Isla was a trim, sharp-featured, 18-year-old A-level student from the new Golden Meadows housing development, with a broad Scottish accent, dark brown eyes and lustrous dark brown hair cut in a very boyish style and somewhat pointed ears, which gave an immediate impression of a Disney Pixie.

Patrick saw from Justin's flushed face and bumbling speech that he wished that he and Isla were more than friends but sympathetically noted that this was unlikely to be reciprocated, as she seemed much more mature and confident for her age than her drooling friend, and if he was any judge of character they would never be more than friends. Sorry Justin!

Patrick picked up from their conversation that they had just two runners in England that weekend whilst "the guvnor" was sending two runners to Dundalk, again, although the prize money was better in England, so he didn't understand why the two that were destined for the all-weather in Ireland were not running here at Southwell this weekend, "makes more sense to me", as Justin, did his best to impart his obvious wealth of knowledge in the hopes of impressing Isla.

Even though the stable had four runners this weekend, it seemed that Justin couldn't see any of them winning, "Don't bother backing any of them chief", chief being Justin's form of address for Patrick once he found out that he was ex-Police, his opinion of their prospects lending further weight to the dubious decision of sending them all that way.

Patrick confessed to knowing little about racing, but the economic realities were the same in any business and he found himself questioning the motives for the long trip, even more so when Justin informed him that this was a common occurrence.

Over the drinks Patrick mentioned Justin's revelation to John and, as it didn't seem like good practice to him, he asked if he had any idea why Adams would consider this was, in fact, good business, particularly if Justin was to be believed, it was a regular occurrence?

Question thirteen, "What is the national airline of Indonesia called?" roared Peter starting section three which this week was on travel, making further conversation impossible.

At the interval after section three of the quiz, Charlie played mother and fetched three steaming bowls of Curry. John leaned close into Patrick and in a barely audible voice whispered, "Come for coffee after morning stables tomorrow, we'll talk properly then", before sitting up straight and tucking into the Curry which was making Charlie's eyes water and nose run, "Hot enough darling?" John laughed.

After an uneventful final round in which he mentally got just seven out of ten, was he preoccupied or were the questions getting harder week by week?
The winners, a team consisting of an accountant and sales manager with their partners calling themselves, Abba 2, he couldn't be bothered to try to think why, scored twenty-seven out of a possible thirty, winning £30 but the jackpot rolled over for another week and now stood at £220, maybe he and the Darby's should start to play?

Patrick had a fitful night's sleep in which he dreamed of Melanie driving his first car, a rusty old grey Vauxhall Viva with no road tax or MOT, to his mother's home in Norfolk, only for her to have moved back to Yorkshire, he never seemed to sleep properly when he'd been drinking Black Sheep, perhaps he'd try a different beer next week.

He woke to the sound of Mrs. Weston singing along to Crystal Gayle's "Don't it make your Brown Eyes Blue" on Ken Bruce's show and realised he had overslept if that is, it was possible to oversleep when you worked for yourself and had nothing to get up for.

"Bugger", he admonished himself, remembering that he was meeting John for a coffee this morning to continue last night's conversation.

He quickly shaved, the smell of his Nivea shaving gel and the feel of the Wilkinson triple-bladed razor effortlessly removing his stubble, quickly waking him before he enjoyed the luxury of an extra few minutes letting the steaming hot shower prepare him for the day.

Mrs. Weston had heard him in the bathroom and he came downstairs to an aromatic mug of black coffee, she had quickly mastered his coffee machine, and with croissants warming in the oven, life was good!

Putting on his Barbour, which was almost obligatory around these parts, and thinking how good it would feel to have a dog to walk, he made for the front door. Just as he was about to leave the phone rang.

"How's my favourite author this morning? the creative juices flowing through your fingers as they dance across your red-hot keyboard bringing a plenitude of wealth for us both I trust?" orated Giles, showing off his customary flowery vocabulary, "In other words, how's it coming along dear boy?"

"OK" lied Patrick, attempting to placate his publisher. It was a call that he had been expecting and was frustrated that he had in fact only started to think about the storyline of his new book in the last few days, he had been so busy with moving house, the strange occurrences, settling in and above all, Melanie.

"I should be able to give you a synopsis in the next week or so", he continued cheerfully. "I'd value your opinion before I get too entrenched in the characters, so why don't I come and see you in the next couple of weeks?"

"Not started yet then?" Giles was experienced in dealing with authors over many years and recognised the language.

"It's your readers your disappointing dear boy, strike whilst the iron's hot eh? don't let it go to waste Patrick, for both our sakes", he continued in a much more serious tone.

Patrick felt like a naughty schoolboy who'd been up before the headmaster but knew that Giles was right and had every reason to expect him to produce the work, he'd have to make a real start soon.

He'd use the walk to see John this morning to think about his new book, which he had already been advised by many would be harder to write than the first and they were right.

The stables were settling down after morning work. The yard was being hosed down, horse's heads peeked out of the open top half of stable doors still excited from their exercise, lads shouting across the yard as they tended their charges and the delicious smell of bacon becoming stronger as he approached the house.

John and Charlie's two black Labradors bounded out to meet him, "Hello", he shouted through the open front door as he patted their heads.

Charlie's face appeared through the kitchen door at the end of the corridor. "Come through Patrick, we're in here", she boomed, quickly retreating.

The kitchen table was almost full with breakfast in full swing, John at the head discussing the performance and progress of the string on the gallops this morning and listening intently to the opinions of his Head Lad, Simon Johnson, and a couple of older work-riders, whilst recording these details in a well-worn notebook held together with a thick, green rubber band, which Patrick thought would be something of a Holy Grail to John.

"Grab a chair Patrick, breakfast?" Charlie retrieved a massive enamel dish half full of bacon, sausages and black pudding from the oven. "How many eggs?" His walk in the crisp morning air had blown away the cobwebs and, despite having quickly devoured his customary croissants before he left home, had given him an appetite, that was another effect of his Thursday night beers.

Chapter 16

The first winter snow of the year began to fall in Vienna as Josef Weismann read the morning's Wiener Zeitung daily newspaper with little enthusiasm.

Nearing his eightieth birthday, the Austrian born solicitor, who had spent over forty years practicing in Bucharest, now worked only a few hours each month looking after his loyal clients, many of whom had become friends.
At his age, he felt it unfair to take on any new clients.

Josef had been a well-respected criminal lawyer in his day and after the war spent many years helping to track down Nazi War Criminals who had been responsible for the deaths of so many of his family and friends in the concentration camps.

Sitting at his favourite corner table in Café Hawelka on Dorotheergasse for his customary elevenses, his thoughts returned to his beloved wife of fifty-two years, Elsa, as the wonderful aroma of the Buchteln yeast buns with a delicious array of jams filled the already busy coffee shop.
Maybe he had decided to visit every day because the aroma reminded him so much of Elsa baking in their tiny kitchen in their first apartment in the Donauinsel district of Vienna after they were first married, or maybe it was somewhere that he could usually get his favourite table at this time of day, he was nowdays a confirmed creature of habit.

The cafe with its green marble topped tables, dark wooden furniture and hat stands, showed off low-hung, spherical, off white glass lights and with pretty, attentive waitresses in white blouses and aprons with black skirts, reminded him of the Vienna of his youth and would not have looked out of place in a Harry Lime film.

Since Elsa's death three years ago after a short battle with cancer, Josef had neither the energy or motivation to carry on working in his adopted home of Bucharest and returned to Vienna, to a small, first floor apartment on Himmelfortstrasse, overlooking the Stadtpark where he would watch the seasons slowly changing in a mood which had of late become increasingly melancholy.

They were never fortunate enough to have the children that Elsa dearly longed for and now she was gone, and his friends, not so many now and mainly still in Bucharest, he was a very lonely man.

His eyes scanned the international news page and hovered over a small item from England which read; "Rumanian Accountant found Murdered". He read the account with increasing concern as the man was named as Miroslav Novotny. He knew this to be the assumed name of his friend and client Pavel Popescu for whom he held a parcel of letters and a large, heavy book together with elaborate instructions for their distribution should he die in unusual circumstances, together with his Will.

He had acted as the defence lawyer for Pavel when he was charged with embezzlement in Bucharest twenty years ago and always believed that he had been innocent of the charges, but the state machine had already decided that they had sufficient evidence, albeit circumstantial, before the trial began and good as Josef was, it was inevitable that Pavel would be found guilty.

Were the government officials in Rumania at that time corrupt? Yes, in the main. Were the judiciary and police forces in the pockets of the Rumanian Mafia? Again, yes, in the main.

He continued to represent clients for many years however, in the belief that without his efforts, many more innocent people would endure the atrocious conditions in Rumanian prisons and succumb to the drug dependencies, ice cold midnight showers and habitual beatings that lead to the Mafia being the good guys when their recruitment offered the only way out.

He was sorry to read this news but at least he now had something to do. He needed to ensure he continued his legal responsibilities to his friend and having finished his Sacher cake he left with an unfamiliar spring in his step to retrieve some of Pavel's documents from his diminishing safety deposit box at the Liechtensteinische Landesbank (Osterreich) AG in Wipplingerstrasse.

Returning to his flat, he sat in his favourite armchair, idly watching a young couple wrapped up in big coats and colourful, matching knitted woollen hats pushing a small child in an expensive looking, modern, dark blue pushchair through the park, the hood which obscured his view of the child already starting to turn white with the covering of light snow and thought of his friend Pavel, wondering just how he had met his death. As usual, at this time of day, his heavy eyes began to close and in a few minutes, he was sound asleep.

When he woke, it was dark and the stark white of the streetlights flooded the room, the hum of the traffic told him it was around five, rush hour. How glad he was that he did not have to contend with trying to get home after work at the same time as everyone else anymore.

He switched on the blue and gold Chinese table lamp next to his chair and re-arranged the cushion before going into the kitchen and putting on the kettle for a coffee, instant nowadays as he thought making coffee just for himself in his old filter jug was not worth the effort. He thought the same about meals and retrieved a frozen lasagna from the small freezer compartment in his outdated fridge for his dinner.

One thing he didn't skimp on was his whisky and poured himself a good measure of his chosen Glenfiddich, which he always drank around this time with his coffee, before sitting at the dining table and opening Pavel's file.

He studied the instructions carefully, methodically reading each line to familiarise himself once again with his late friend's wishes.

Having read all the documents a second time, he took a notepad and pen from the rolled-top writing bureau ready to begin immediately after his gourmet dinner. He searched the fridge for salad to have with his dinner and found half of a limp lettuce and a the remains of a soggy cucumber, before deciding that he would settle just for the lasagna and perhaps pick up some fresh food from the excellent indoor market tomorrow, after all, he didn't feel so hungry and had work to do.

The first call the following morning was to the Police in South Yorkshire who had found poor Pavel's body to confirm the fact of his death.

After successfully negotiating an eternity of pressing numbers to be "put through to the right department", he spoke to a polite female voice.

"South Yorkshire Police, how may I help you?" was the response.
"I need to speak to whoever is in charge of the reported death of Pavel Popescu please", replied Josef.
"I'll see if I can find someone, who's calling please?"
"My name is Josef Weissman, I am an attorney-at-law here in Vienna".
"One moment Mr. Weissman".

After a few minutes of uninspiring music and a recorded message saying that the police valued your call and thanks for waiting,

"Good morning Mr. Weissman, I'm DS Wakefield, you are making enquiries about Pavel Popescu?"

"Good morning DS Wakefield, I am Josef Weissman, Pavel Popescu's solicitor, I have read in the newspaper here in Vienna this morning that you have found Pavel's body, is that correct?"

"Yes Mr. Weissman I'm afraid so, but what you can tell me about it," asked Wakefield.

"Well firstly can I ask how sure you are that the body you have found is that of my client?"

"One hundred percent, we identified him from his fingerprints on his police record in Rumania".

"In that case DS Wakefield, I will need to speak to you again soon".

"Hang on a minute, what is it you can tell me, Mr. Weissman? I'll obviously treat everything in strict confidence.".

"I am sure you will, but I am afraid that it must wait a short while until I have made a few more enquiries, then I am sure you will be pleased to receive items that Pavel has left for the police. Goodbye, DS Wakefield, I'll be in touch soon. Oh, and just in case something should happen to me in the meantime I will leave a package with your name on it, please write this down, it will be waiting in your name at the Liechtensteinische Landesbank (Osterreich) AG in Wipplingerstrasse in Vienna. Please keep this information to yourself, DS Wakefield, it is very important that the authorities or police in Rumania do not hear of this conversation, you understand me?"

"Of course Mr. Weissman, but this is a murder enquiry and I need you to tell me what you know".

"All in good time detective," after which Josef put the receiver down.

Josef's first action according to Pavel's instructions was to satisfy himself that Pavel's daughter Ana-Maria was alive and safe. When Pavel had been imprisoned, his wife Gretchen returned to Vienna with Ana-Maria and immediately sought a divorce. She re-married in just two years and Ana-Maria took the name of her mother's new husband, Heinrich Fischer.
Josef had no idea what had become of Ana-Maria but would need to find out. He knew however that she had a son, Pavel's grandson, Peter, and he had been quite easy to keep track of.
He was now, at just twenty-six, Principal Cellist with the Vienna Philharmonic Orchestra and Josef had seen him play on several occasions.

As Peter was playing the following Saturday night at the Wiener Musikverein's Golden Hall, Josef called and made arrangements with the stage manager to speak to him after the performance, stressing that he was a solicitor and it was an "urgent and personal matter".

Josef retrieved a brown suit from the wardrobe in the small bedroom and polished his best brown brogues, old, but as comfortable as carpet slippers and made his way down the cold, stone stairs to the front of the apartment building to hail a taxi.

After a wonderful performance of Haydn's Die 7 letzten Worte unseres Erlösers am Kreuze and Luigi Cherubini's Missa solemnis, Josef made his way to the stage door and his appointment with Peter.

Josef complimented him on the performance before suggesting that they moved to the nearby Hotel Imperial bar where he would explain the urgency of the meeting with the solicitor who he had never met before.

Ordering a large malt whisky for himself and a tonic water for Peter, they sat at a small table at the end of the bar which was fortunately fairly quiet, the Saturday night revelers still out in the city.
Josef introduced himself and retrieved a pristine white business card from a silver and gold engraved card holder which said quite simply; Josef Weissman, Attorney-at-Law together with his phone number.

"What's this all about", inquired Peter, intrigued, to say the least.
"I know you don't know me but I know all about you. Tell me, what do you know of your grandfather?" started Josef, wondering what the reply would be.
"I never knew my grandparents, they died in the war".
"I'm sorry Peter, but that is what you were told to protect you. Your grandmother, your mother's mother, died many years ago that's true, but your grandfather died recently in England.
I knew your grandfather well, as well as being a friend he was also a client of mine in Bucharest, it is a long story and perhaps I will have the time to tell you someday, but for now I can tell you that he left detailed instructions for me to carry out on his death.

Firstly, however, I am required to assure myself that both you and your mother are "safe and well", his words you understand. You I can see are well but I have lost all touch with your mother, Ana-Marie, that's her name, isn't it?"

"Yes, it is. Forgive me Mr. Weissman", a confused Peter asked looking at the business card, "but why would I be told that they were dead and what do you want to know about my mother for?"

"I'm sure you have a lot of questions and in good time I will be able to tell you everything I'm sure, but for now I need to know that your mother is well?"

"Yes, I spoke with her on Wednesday last".

"That is good. Would you prefer that I told her about your grandfather or...?"

"No, I'll go and see her. I have some questions of my own for her", Peter replied abruptly.

"Good, good, then I need to get on and deal with the rest of the instructions. If she has any questions, then please tell her to call me. Oh, and I also have your grandfather's Will but I am instructed that this must remain unread for the moment".

Getting up to leave, Josef asked, "To save more cloak and dagger approaches perhaps you would be good enough to give me your phone number so that I can keep you informed of events?"

He scribbled Peter's mobile number in his small pocket diary, he had no use of anything larger nowadays.

Satisfied that the first instruction had been completed he stepped out into the cold wet night and hailed a taxi for home, his work would now begin.

"I hope to do as you wished very soon my old friend," he told himself as he settled himself into the rear of the spacious Canary Yellow Mercedes taxi emblazoned on both sides with Taxi 40100.

Chapter 17

Meadowhall Shopping Centre was busy, but then on a Saturday at 11.00 o'clock in the morning, when wasn't it.

Next to the M1 motorway in Sheffield with its own mainline station, bus station and with modern Supertrams connecting to almost all parts of Sheffield, this had been the shopping destination of choice for people of South Yorkshire and beyond for over twenty years, and visitors regularly travelled as much as seventy miles to shop, or even enjoy the many restaurants and multi-screen cinema complex, all housed under the same roof with its distinctive green and blue framed, glass dome.

It was also next to the River Don, which had been skillfully diverted to allow the building of the complex and was now forced between manmade retaining walls before returning to natural banks, covered in brambles, weeds and litter as it made its way beneath the giant bridge carrying the road to Rotherham on the first level and the busy M1 on the upper level.

The footbridge to the mainline railway and bus stations crossed the river by way of a glass covered walkway high above the river, unlike the time that is when it flooded in 2002 when it seemed you could almost touch the dirty, brown waters carrying a veritable mountain of debris as it raced on its way beneath the road bridge.

Arthur and Enid Worsley from Rotherham were making their way over the footbridge, having arrived on the overcrowded, noisy Northern Rail train from Rotherham Central, for their usual Saturday morning visit to buy a few weekend treats from the excellent Marks and Spencer Food Hall, to supplement their weekly, Friday ASDA shop, when Arthur happened to glance down to his left at the thick, dark, muddy waters of the Don when he saw what looked to be a naked body floating slowly away from the bridge.

"Look at that Enid, is it what I think it is?"
"Ooh Arthur, it looks like it is" replied Enid concentrating on the object, but Arthur had wasted no time as he immediately dialed 999 on his old Nokia mobile phone,
"Police, Fire or Ambulance?"
"All three I think," said the slightly flustered, retired steelworker.
"What's your name sir?" enquired the operator.
"Arthur Worsley, why?"
"And is this your phone your calling from sir?"
"'Of course it is, who else's would it be?"
"What's the nature of the emergency Mr. Worsley?" came a slightly friendlier yet professional reply.
"There's a body int' Don at Meadowhall, just past footbridge, I'm looking at it now".
"Stay where you are Arthur, the Police are on their way and they may need to talk to you".
"That's buggered Satday up, am supposed to be going to Hillsborough this aft! I'll nivver mek it nar".
Arthur had regained both his composure and his accent.

Five minutes later three Police cars and an Ambulance, with blue lights flashing and sirens wailing, made their way towards Meadowhall Interchange rail and bus station from the direction of Sheffield City Centre.

"Looking for Arthur Worsley", shouted one of the two constables now fighting their way through the crowd of onlookers who had gathered on the footbridge to see what the fuss was all about.

"Over here", shouted Arthur and proceeded to show the constables where he had seen the body floating, although it had now disappeared.

Almost on cue, however, the body resurfaced about 400 metres further away and one of the constables radioed the information to his colleagues who were scouring the river and banking but were too near to the bridge.

Once they had located the body, the roads around the heaving Shopping Centre were quickly sealed off and the body was pulled from the river just before the bend, after which it disappeared down one of the weirs on its way to Rotherham and beyond making recovery, as it was certain that by now anyone in the water for that length of time would be dead, much more difficult.

"DI Bradshaw", answering her radio and hoping that it was nothing serious as she was off duty in a couple of hours and hadn't had a weekend off since her week in Tenerife in July.

"You're needed at Meadowhall boss, there's a body in the river", replied control Sammi Lindley, manning the desk for the day.

"OK, can you find Wakefield and Stanhope and have them meet me there?" she replied, resigning herself to the fact that this was another Saturday when her plans were going to have to be changed, c'est la vie!
"Yes Boss".
"And tell them not to make any plans for the day, I'm sure they'll love you for that".
"Thanks, Boss", Sammi replied knowing the reception she would receive to the call she was about to make.

Even with blue lights and sirens on, trying to get through the snarled-up traffic caused by the road closures was a challenge, and when she arrived twenty minutes later, officers awaiting her arrival had tried to shield the body from onlookers, whilst at the same time looking along the riverbank to look for any signs of where the body had entered.
"Right then, what have we got constable".
"Female, naked, her face has been badly beaten and both of her hands are missing Ma'am".
"Not looking like suicide then boss", chirped up DS Wakefield from behind having followed Bradshaw down the banking.

"Get a CSI team down here as soon as possible James, I'll call Lewis, if he can spare the time".
"Not going to be easy to identify her with her hands cut off and her face in that state boss".
"Where's Stanhope? Best keep her away from the scene until the CSI team have finished, I don't want her throwing up all over the place".
"Come on boss, we've all been there. Anyway, she's got to get used to it"

Fifteen minutes later, three white-suited CSIs had erected then entered a white tent to preserve the scene and shield the body from view, although Bradshaw was very sceptical about what evidence they would find other than the body itself, and what damage a shower of rain would do she couldn't quite see. It did, however, have the effect of dispersing the crowd on the footbridge as Arthur gave his details and was told to expect a visit later in the day to take a full statement.

"Interrupted my golf again DI Bradshaw, I should get you to contribute to my bloody green fees if you carry on like this or is there any chance you could just catch the bloody killer instead and leave me in peace?" said the brusque, ginger haired pathologist Dr. Lewis with his usual morose manner, as he walked down the banking still in his red trousers, black Footglove golf shoes and MacGregor tartan sweater.

Bradshaw decided not to interrupt Doctor Misery whilst he gave the body a cursory examination.

"Any chance of a time of death? Best guess will be a start".

"Difficult to estimate given that she's been in the water but probably less than 24 hours, however, I won't know any more until I get her back to the lab and no it won't be before Monday morning. Now let me get on and I might manage 9 holes later"

"I want all reports of missing persons in the last seven days and her description circulated to all Yorkshire and Derbyshire forces Wakefield, not easy with the face battered like that I know ", said Bradshaw, knowing that the first 24 hours were vital in any murder investigation and if Lewis's first impression was right, at least they could get off to a flying start.

There was little else that Lewis could tell her other than she was approximately five feet five inches and maybe East European "but maybe not", possibly on drugs judging by the needle marks on her arm "but maybe not", but there was a distinctive tattoo on her neck, under the hairline, of an angel standing on a cloud which carried the name "Katya", could it be her name or that of a child?

But two murders in a very short time, but with different MOs, only the scale of brutality appeared the same, were they looking for two different killers or were they connected. If Lewis was right and she was Eastern European surely that would tie them together? They had identified the first murder as a professional hit and this looked anything but a simple rape or fight gone wrong.

They were sure that Weissman would have more to tell them about Novotny aka Popescu when they next spoke but if she was Eastern European, surely it was too much of a coincidence that they both ended up dead in South Yorkshire, and such a short time apart.

Reports of the body were broadcast initially on Radio Sheffield and later in the day on the TV station's local news sections, Look North and Calendar and were able to give a description of the girl, height, colouring, approximate age and most importantly the distinctive tattoo.

It was eleven-thirty that evening that the anonymous call was received by South Yorkshire Police via the Crimewatch number confirming that Chloe, who worked at Veronica's, was missing since Friday and matched that description and yes, she did have a tattoo with the name "Katya" on her neck. Katya was her daughter.

The caller hung up before giving any more information but the recording was made against a background of heavy music, could it have been from a Disco or Massage Parlour?

Chapter 18

"If Melanie's up this weekend do you fancy a drink or a curry on Saturday?" said Dan, catching Patrick just as he was getting out of the shower. Why is it phones were programmed to ring every time you entered a bath or shower?

"Yes great, we'd like that, where are you thinking?"
"There's a really good place in Northallerton, The Kingfisher in the Market Place, it's easy to find, we've been a few times and believe me Nayna knows the difference between good and great Indian food and being a woman, the service has to be spot on as well"
"I know Melanie will be pleased to see you both again, so we'll see you there about 8 o'clock then?"
"OK, see you, Saturday, take care"
Patrick thought this would be a good opportunity to discuss his suspicions about Adams' uneconomic trips with Mullins Transport and would try to broach the subject if he could get Dan on his own.
Melanie arrived on Friday evening with the aroma of freshly baked bread and freshly brewed coffee making the kitchen very welcoming, little wonder estate agents believe this is what makes a house more saleable.
"We're going out with Dan and Nanya tomorrow night for an Indian if that's OK?" suddenly awakening to the fact that maybe he should have checked with Melanie first, but she and Nanya did get on.
"Great, I like Nanya and it's a long time since we went out for a curry".

"Fancy a walk to the Margrave for a drink before supper," asked Patrick, knowing that he would not want to be out too long as an early night was far more tempting.

"OK, what's for supper anyway?" the ever-hungry Melanie replied.

"I've just done us a simple Beef and Guinness casserole with a few veg and I've made some granary bread to go with it, but if you're really hungry I can pop a few mustard dumplings in when we get back, it'll be ready in a couple of hours?"

"Sounds lovely älskling, don't want to eat too much before bed, though," she replied with a chuckle in her voice.

"That's what I call a start to the weekend," grinned Patrick, receiving a punch to the arm for his cheek, before wishing he hadn't suggested going to the pub.

Walking hand-in-hand through the village with Melanie wrapped up in her white woollen short coat and matching knitted hat, skin tight black cords and knee-length black high-heeled boots, the clear night sky seemingly full of stars shimmering in the cold night air and with the promise of spending the whole weekend together, Patrick felt truly blessed.

The Margrave was busy. Evening stables had finished and the lads and girls were seemingly looking forward to the weekend, judging by the wall of noise that hit them as Melanie opened the door, the warmth of the fire and the crowd like stepping into an oven.

"Pint of Black Sheep and a dry white wine?" enquired Angela Castle, shouting to be heard through the heads at the crowded bar before Melanie had had chance to even unbutton her coat.

"Beginning to feel like we're regulars," commented Melanie before a shout of "Evening chief" made Patrick turn to face a grinning tousle-haired Justin who looked as though he was about to burst, "Have a little tickle on Anna's Pride at Wolverhampton tomorrow night Chief, a pal tells me it should walk it", confided Justin knowing that a pint would be paid for him at the bar shortly plus a reward should his tip win, which more often than not it did, would follow soon.

Two drinks later by which time Patrick couldn't take either his eyes or hands off Melanie, they decided that supper should be ready and stepped out into the crisp, frosty evening for the walk home, Melanie looping her arm through Patrick's and snuggling up close to him.

The warmth of the kitchen and the smell of the food cooking in the AGA as they walked in, made Patrick's stomach rumble and seated in front of the fire with the casserole and crusty bread on trays they made short work of their supper. Leaving the trays with the dirty plates on the kitchen worktop Melanie led an impatient Patrick hurriedly upstairs where he lifted her and laid her on the bed as she tore at his jeans fastening, freeing his manhood as he urgently tried to pull down her skin-tight trousers and skimpy black lace panties and enter her, not even having time to remove her sweater and bra.

After climaxing together, which was something that always happened from the second or third time they made love, as if their bodies knew instinctively what the other needed, they lay in each other's arms, when Melanie began giggling like a naughty child, realising that although they both wanted to make love so desperately that they had not spoken since finishing supper, Patrick still had his jeans and underpants around his ankles, not very elegant, and a vision that tickled Melanie's sense of humour and sent her into fits of laughter.

Saturday morning was greeted with blue skies and fleeting white pillows as the wind had increased overnight, rustling the remnants of the autumn leaves before sending them scurrying across the driveway as Patrick and Melanie walked to the village for the morning paper and a few other groceries.

They had decided to drive into York to choose more furniture and soft furnishings for the Farm and Patrick had already agreed mentally to simply go along with Melanie's choice, not least because if she had a free choice it would probably mean that they would be home much sooner. He drove home with the car full of new cushions and a copy of an order for two new, burgundy leather Chesterfield sofas for the lounge to replace his favourite old one, his mild protestations almost ignored with a "you told me to choose, or have you changed your mind?" and not wishing to find out the consequences of even answering.

Melanie came down at 6.30pm showered and dressed in tight jeans and a designer jumper in autumn russet with appliqué black and brown leaves to the front, her hair swept back and held with a tortoiseshell clip and looking a million dollars.

"Wow!" Patrick exclaimed as he saw her, "are you sure you want to go out tonight?"

"Of course, but it was your idea", she replied laughingly.

The half hour drive to Northallerton, listening to Magic FM was full of idle conversation but came around to how much they enjoyed spending the weekends together and Patrick wondered whether they would find a way to make the arrangement more permanent.

Finding a parking space in the Market Place they spied Dan and Nanya waiting for them outside The Kingfisher and Melanie realised how hungry she was, having not eaten since their brunch at eleven that morning.

Hope Nanya was right about the food she thought to herself.

Handshakes and kisses concluded they sat in the bar with pints of Kingfisher lager, what else, and two Sauvignon Blanc for the girls, who gratefully took the proffered menus.

"What do you recommend Nanya? Dan tells me you're the expert", asked Patrick.

"Not sure about expert but each time we come I always order the Prawn Puri to start and they do a fabulous Nariyal Chicken which is in a hot coconut sauce but it might not be your choice".

"If you recommend it, that's good enough for me" Patrick pronounced.

"Me too", agreed Melanie closing the bright blue and orange menu. "What about you Dan?"
"I'm not a hot curry man, Chicken Tikka Masala is as much as I can manage", confided Dan to a chorus of laughter.

The meal was delicious, the service outstanding and the restaurant busy, but unobtrusive, with conversation flowing easily all evening, and as they left for home the girls agreed that next time they would come over and have dinner at the Farm, and they could possibly stay over and make a weekend of it.

The conversation with Dan regarding Adams and Mullins would have to wait.

Without the opportunity to speak to Dan, Patrick resolved to investigate Adams' activities himself as soon as the occasion presented itself. After all, it was only as he had done when he was in the force, but this time there would be no back up but then again, no one to cock it up either.
Patrick checked the racing in Ireland for the weekend and sure enough, there was a Friday evening meeting at Dundalk, Ireland's only all-weather course.
He looked at the card on the website and with the prize money guaranteed at 7000 Euros for every race, he could see that if Adams' horses won or were even placed then he may make a profit, so why was Justin so het up about it?

Only one way to find out, so with his metallic blue Range Rover now being a well recognised vehicle around Abbot's Meadow, particularly with his plate of PL12MET, he rented a Ford Mondeo Ghia X from Enterprise Car Rental in Malton and booked himself onto the 13.50hrs Irish Ferries ferry from Holyhead to Dublin, hoping that this was the route that Mullins would take with Adams' horses, being the most logical.

5am on Thursday, Patrick sat in his hire car in a lay-by on the westbound A64 just outside of Malton, waiting for Mullins transporter to pass on its way over the Pennines towards Holyhead in North Wales.

He reflected that this reminded him of stakeout duties in his early days in CID in the Met, the difference being that here he was not following orders and he did not have a partner to keep him awake if it became too tiring.
He had however bought a supply of oranges, as his first partner had told him that the smell of fresh orange peel was thought to wake the senses, something he had remembered and found in the past that it worked.

Just after 6.00am the transporter passed and as he knew the route they were taking, even if he had guessed wrongly and they were travelling to Belfast via Liverpool they would travel on the M62, but that would mean crossing the border into the Republic and he didn't believe this would be their preferred option, so he had no need to stay too close as he knew they would be on the same ferry.

His main question was though, if the horses were not being sent purely for racing purposes, what were they being sent for and who would they contact during the journey there or back? One thing he was sure of was that it would happen, if at all, once they had crossed the Irish Sea, not in the UK.

Patrick followed the Transporter at a distance, not too difficult as it was considerably larger than a car and travelled at 60 mph or less until it pulled into Birch Services. The first problem that he hadn't envisaged was that the transporter would pull into the HGV parking section whilst he could only pull into the section specifically reserved for cars.

Being 8.15am on a Thursday, a normal business day, both parking areas were busy with business drivers taking breaks from early starts or truck drivers having driven through the night getting their heads down in their sleeper cabs. The cafeteria was flooded with drivers hungrily devouring large Full English breakfasts; Bacon, Sausage, Black Pudding, Beans, Tomatoes, Eggs and Fried Bread, and queues of people with loaded trays searching the busy dining area for seats when they became available.

Fortunately, Patrick spotted the red hair of McLaughlin in the cafeteria queue and guessed that Bălan had stayed with the horses, which was confirmed when he watched him buy hot breakfast sandwiches and coffee in cardboard cups to take out.

Knowing that he could soon catch up with the Transporter if they left straight away and ate breakfast in the cab, Patrick ordered Bacon and eggs with toast and a black coffee, hoping the caffeine would help mitigate the 4am alarm.

Having eaten his breakfast as fast as he could without guaranteeing indigestion, he walked quickly to his car and pulled out onto the Motorway, scouring the HGV Park as he left to ensure the Transporter was still there.

There was no sign.

Still convinced they were En-route to Holyhead, he hoped so as he had already purchased his ticket online, he reckoned that he had at least 2 hours to catch them up, which would be ample.

By the time he passed the Motorway sign for junction 20A Chester, North Wales, Runcorn and Manchester South and despite being held up by an accident closing lane three when two cars had decided to have a fight, Patrick was getting concerned. Surely he would have caught up with them by now? He had little choice but to continue through to Holyhead. Staying on the A55 and passing Colwyn Bay, Bangor and onto the Isle of Anglesey, there was still no sign. They must have turned off shortly after leaving the services and that left the whole of Lancashire and Greater Manchester as potential rendezvous points if indeed there was a rendezvous point, and for what purpose, Patrick could not even begin to imagine.

Parking up in a lay-by outside of Holyhead, he decided to wait, as if they did not travel on the ferry then he had wasted his journey but he still had three hours before sailing.

The temptation to close his eyes for a few minutes was almost too great but although he had managed a few hours' sleep, 4am was very early and he peeled an orange under his nose, fighting to stay awake, knowing full well that if he closed his eyes he would have no idea if the Transporter had passed him or not or even when he would wake up.

Opening the windows to let in the cold, fresh, salty sea air he wondered why he thought that he had to get involved, after all, he was no longer in the job and the Police were far better equipped than he was.

Almost two hours later he saw the familiar livery of the Transporter in his driver's door mirror and instinctively looked to his left as it passed him.

"Yes!" he said punching the air in triumph as he knew that he was right about their plans until he realised that all he had guessed was the ferry that they were taking, not why they were travelling or even where they had been since they left Birch Services. "Need to get a grip Spencer" he chastised himself.

Coming back to earth with a bump he followed them into the Terminal Waiting Area and parked amidst a mass of HGVs from seemingly every part of Europe and a much smaller number of private cars, many with Irish plates.

The huge Irish Ferries MV Epsilon was more like a cruise ship than the ferries he remembered when travelling with the school to France for a week, and loading was very slick and organised, taking much less time than he had expected. He was berthed on a different deck to the HGV but this time, he had no fears about losing them, at least before they reached Dublin anyway.

The journey was calm and was anything but the crossing he expected at this time of year and he spent the first hour of the crossing dozing in one of the large, comfortable, blue imitation leather seats in the small cinema. Waking up feeling groggy he bought a coffee from the Cafe and took it up on deck to clear the cobwebs and come around fully, not knowing when he would get the chance to sleep again.

The journey was uneventful; he saw McLaughlin's red hair over the heads of a few diners in Cafe Lafayette but there was no sign of Bălan.

As no one was allowed to stay below decks when the ship sailed Patrick wondered where he could be as it seemed logical that the two drivers would at least eat together.

Below decks Bălan was not eating.

He had been helped by a deck security supervisor, Eamonn Laugherty, to berth the Transporter adjacent to an Irish Artic belonging to Emerald Isle Transport, the largest transport business in Ireland with Emerald Green and White livery proudly sporting a Shamrock logo with the slogan "Serving the World".

Laugherty was ostensibly checking the fastenings on the vehicles on deck 3 when Bălan, jumped down from the cab and nodding to the security supervisor, knocked on the cab door of the Artic.

Jumping down and quietly unlocking the rear cargo doors of the vehicle, Stephen O'Connor, opened up the concealed space amongst the pallets in the back of the truck.

Bălan, pistol in hand, waved two teenage girls from the Transporter cab and ensured that they were safely locked in the back of the Emerald Isle truck before taking a khaki coloured duffel bag from O'Connor and concealing the bag and himself back in the cab of the Transporter.

Business finished.

The rest of the day was frustrating for Patrick as he followed the Transporter, now with both McLaughlin and Bălan aboard, to Dundalk where from a distance and through binoculars he watched Adams' two horses being unloaded and stabled for the night,

Bălan and McLaughlin carrying identical duffel bags walked the short distance to the "Rising Sun" B&B where they disappeared inside.

Although it was only 7.30pm, Patrick drove until he found The Castle Bar on Seatown, a fine old Irish pub, and having used their toilet facilities, thought it only right to try a pint of Guinness.

He drove back and parked in sight of the Rising Sun where after eating the sandwiches he thoughtfully bought on the ferry, he retrieved a thick, new sleeping bag from the boot and was soon fast asleep on the fully reclined seat of the luxurious Mondeo, setting his mobile alarm for 5am.

Fully awake he realised why the B&B was called the Rising Sun, as the sun, soon after dawn, shone directly onto the pebble dashed front of the building, giving an impression of being a lovely rose-pink colour instead of the dull grey which all the buildings in this part of Ireland seemed to be.

The two drivers left just after 11am and made their way to the racecourse where they spent the day drinking coffee and smoking, until racing on the all-weather track started at 5pm. Fortunately, Adams' horses were running in the first and third races so they would hopefully be on their way home in time to catch the 9pm sailing.

As Justin, had predicted the horses finished 5th and 7th respectively and were soon loaded and ready for the journey home.

Patrick was now fully alert as he was sure something would happen before they boarded the ferry, but having followed Bălan and McLaughlin, he managed to squeeze a booking onto the 9pm ferry, which was very busy given that it was Friday evening and people were hoping to spend the weekend at various locations in the UK.

Having followed them back to Malton at a steady 60 mph with no detours, he was disappointed that he could find nothing that would explain the reason for such a wasted trip.

Wasted in terms of both time and money, his as well as Adams'. There had to be something he was missing.

The only mystery was where had they been on the journey over to Holyhead?

Chapter 19

The December snow that had forced the abandonment of all racing in the UK since last Wednesday was forecasted to last for at least another five days and threatened to force Melanie to give up her plans to stay at Patrick's over the weekend.

Her colleagues at the BBC however, had assured her that it should stop by early evening Saturday and, although cold and frosty, Sunday should be ideal for a crisp, winter walk, if of course, she could get there. The AA website convinced her that all roads were passable and armed with this information she decided to travel on Friday as arranged.

She would have been disappointed to have had to change her plans as Abbot's Meadow in winter, particularly leading up to Christmas, took on an almost magical manifestation of everything that was wonderful about this special period with the people seeming outwardly even more friendly, the atmosphere in The Margrave becoming all that a quintessential English pub should be and together with the snow, Melanie was sure that it would remind her of happy childhood Christmases in her native Sweden.

Seemingly a lot of people had decided to stay indoors and as such the traffic, instead of being heavier as people slowed down as they were unprepared to take risks on the potentially icy surfaces, was in fact lighter than most Fridays and she arrived as Patrick was uncorking a bottle of Chateau Neuf du Pape believing he would have another hour to let it breathe before she arrived.

Melanie flung herself at Patrick and kissed him passionately before announcing she was going for a bath.

"What's for supper älskling?" Melanie was hungry, as ever.

"Italian, that OK?"

"Perfect, I'll be down soon", she replied over her shoulder as she tripped lightly towards the stairs.

Melanie reappeared wrapped in Patrick's thick, Autumn Brown toweling bathrobe which dwarfed her petite body and made her look even more desirable if that was possible. The log fire was raging and with her favourite Vanilla scented Yankee Candles lighting the room with a subdued, restful flicker she curled up on the end of the huge sofa with her feet tucked under her and cupping a glass of the full-bodied Burgundy in both hands was instantly both relaxed and excited about the weekend ahead.

Supper was eaten at the end of the large farmhouse table, instead of on trays on their knees in front of the fire, and she noted that the other end was strewn with pages of notes and typed sheets of A4 paper. It looked as though he had actually been working this week, Giles would be pleased!

Not only had he been working, but either he or Mrs. Weston had also been learning to cook as this was obviously a homemade Lasagne, and although she was so hungry she would almost have eaten anything, it was terrific, though they may regret the amount of garlic in the morning.

"How would you fancy putting up some Christmas decorations tomorrow?" he asked tentatively.

"Do you have any?"

"Err, No".

"OK, we'll drive into York and do a bit of shopping in the morning and buy some, then decorate after lunch and we can decide what we are doing over Christmas".

"OK but I'd like to be back to go for a drink in the pub after tea", replied Patrick.

Despite having been together for four years, they had rarely spent much time together at Christmas in the past as Patrick was always busy working on some case or other, so Melanie had usually volunteered to cover the programmes for presenters who had families and so had worked most days over the Christmas period including, for the past three years, Christmas Day itself.

"Any pudding?" she asked getting up from the table and returning to the comfort of the sofa after holding out her wine glass for a refill.

"Tiramisu or me?" he replied lowering his voice into what he perceived to be seductive mode, merely raising a raucous laugh from his radiant partner.

"I'll have both please, but the pudding first", mimicking his seductive tone which somehow seemed exceedingly sexy when she used it.

The Tiramisu was delicious, though again, obviously not made by Patrick.

He stacked the dishwasher and joined her with another glass of wine before he broached the subject of Christmas.

"Will you be working over Christmas again this year?"

"Will you?" she replied but instead of being said reproachfully was almost playful.

"Not necessarily now I'm my own boss, I can put in some extra hours before and after the holiday. I've already made a lot of progress this week and even Giles is pleased for a change".

"Well, in that case, it's a good job that I've told David (the Director of Programmes) that I'm taking Christmas and New Year off as I've worked the last 4 in a row".

"Brilliant", he replied, with an excitement in his voice that let her know that he meant it. "Will you spend it here?"

"Yes, but I would like us to visit my family sometime over the holiday as I don't get to see them much nowadays and I know Melissa will be there with her new boyfriend".

"You said "us" to visit them, do you want me to come?"

As their lives were so disparate it was somehow never the right time to meet the parents and so although Melanie's family knew all about Patrick, they had never actually met, which was ridiculous somehow, given the way that he felt about her and the length of time they had been together.

"Yes, I think meeting my family is well overdue, don't you?"

"OK, it'll be ...", he started to say and paused as if trying to find the right words.

"It'll be what?" she pressed.

"I was going to say it'll be just like a real couple, Christmas together, meeting the family, I hope I can live up to their expectations."

"So do I!" she giggled. "But I've really been looking forward to spending Christmas together and just hoped you were too?"

"I was thinking the same but was a bit scared to ask in case you said no".

"Idiot", was all the reply he needed as he moved over beside her on her sofa and kissed her long and passionately before whispering in her ear, "I love you"

"Jag älskar dig också (I love you too) she whispered in his ear before taking him by the hand and leading him towards the stairs, allowing the open bathrobe to fall as they walked, Patrick scooped her up and carried her naked in a fireman's lift, instantly sending her into a fit of uncontrollable laughter and thumping his back in mock protest.

The weekend continued as it has started, with the two of them excitedly hanging the car full of Christmas decorations, which had made the day of the shop assistant in Brown's department store in York, who presumably had never sold such an order.

They had bought the most expensive door ring from the Christmas Market, made of conifer and holly branches with berries, pine cones, silk poinsettias, bright red and gold bows and scarlet and frosted white baubles with a cheap plastic "Merry Christmas" apparently being shouted by an ebullient, rotund Father Christmas, but somehow it just looked right and Melanie wasted no time in hanging their first Christmas decoration on the front door, promising a warm welcome to all friends and neighbours who cared to call this holiday period.

Whilst Melanie got to grips with the decorations, Patrick raced off to the Black Bull Farm Shop as he had seen the "Christmas Trees For Sale" sign as they returned from York, returning an hour later with an eight-foot tree which he was a shade frustrated to find needed to be soaked in a large bucket of water for a day before bringing indoors to be decorated.
"Ah well, that's a job for tomorrow", he sighed as Melanie turned to hide a grin realising that he was just like a child in a sweet shop, she had never seen this side of him in all the time they had been together.

Buttered crumpets, toasted on the log burner with the door open and using Patrick's homemade, or was it improvised, wire toasting fork reminded her again of her childhood when she would visit her grandparents' home for the holidays and her grandad would toast them while grandma lavished farm-fresh butter on them. For a moment, she was back there hardly hearing Patrick ask if she wanted a cup of tea or coffee.
"Oh, sorry, tea please", she replied dreamily.

After the exertions of the day and with the warmth of the flickering fire, they both closed their eyes and snoozed in each other's arms on her sofa.

Waking with a start he took a few seconds to realise where he was. It was pitch black outside but in the pale glow of the outside light, he could see that it was snowing again.
"Hey Cinderella, come on its six o'clock", as he woke her by kissing her forehead, "Are we going out?"

"Umm, in a while, just let me come around. I must have needed that; I couldn't keep my eyes open".
"Well, we didn't get much sleep last night, did we?"
"Complaining?"
"Definitely not, I would happily have had no sleep at all".
"What do you fancy doing tonight, it's snowing again?"
"Let's go for a steady walk to the pub, at least it will wake us both up".
"OK, I'm going for a hot shower, coming?"
"No. You go first or we'll never get there!"

Wrapped up in chunky sweaters under their Barbour's and wearing wellingtons as the road was covered in snow once again, the walk to Margrave was quiet and they didn't see a soul until they opened the door, when it seemed the whole of Abbot's Meadow must have decided to avail themselves of Peter's roaring log fire and it took five minutes to get served even though as usual Angela has seen them arrive and smiled warmly through the waiting customers who thronged the bar.

"Usual?" came the shout as the noise levels were spirited even for a Saturday night.
"Yes please". It really did feel like he had lived here for ages.
"It's Sam's 18th Birthday so they're all celebrating with her. Don't think they'll last too much longer though, they've been in since four o'clock," Angela explained as she pulled Patrick's pint of Black Sheep as Melanie looked around for any spare seats.

Sitting in an alcove towards the rear of the pub Patrick noticed John Darby frantically waving to him and nearly knocking over Charlotte's red wine as he did so.

"Looks like we've got a seat. Come on I'll introduce you", as he led Melanie over to the Darby's table.

"Hello John, Charlie, this is Melanie, my partner". After the introductions, Charlie squeezed up to John to make a seat for Melanie next to her.

"Nice to meet you at last Melanie, we've heard so much about you".

"All good I hope", she beamed.

"Of course, and John listens to your programme over breakfast after morning stables."

"Sam works for us so we've opened a tab behind the bar, that's what I was waving for, to tell you to put your drinks on the tab", explained John.

"I'll get you next time", Patrick laughed.

The conversation flowed very easily and as expected the crowd started to thin out around eight-thirty with many shouts of "Cheers Governor", as the grateful and inebriated stable hands left to make their way home together.

After Charlie and Melanie had managed to share two more bottles of Peter's most expensive Cabernet Sauvignon, with Melanie trying to teach Charlie inappropriate Swedish words which they both seemed to find hilarious when she tried to repeat them, they decided to walk back together as they would have to pass Oaktree Farm anyway and the odds of finding a taxi on a night like this was remote, to say the least.

Wrapping up it was strange that all four had the same colour and style of Barbour and all four had the ubiquitous Hunter wellies.

Realising as soon as they said goodnight to Peter and Angela and the few customers who were still left that they had not eaten since the crumpets at tea time, Patrick suggested they call at the "Golden Pagoda", which was still open and take a Chinese back to Oaktree to which a well-oiled Charlie slurred that she was starving.
"You know what the lads call this place don't you Melanie? The Flying Arsehole", before laughing hysterically at herself and causing the others to join in.

"Nice door ring Melanie" Charlie acknowledged as they went into the cosy kitchen.
"Looks to have a woman's style", the cold air seemed to have quickly sobered her up.
After an hour of good company and easy conversation making short work of Salt and Pepper Ribs, Chilli Chicken Wings, Sweet and Sour Chicken and Filet of Beef Cantonese with far too much egg fried rice, Patrick suggested a nightcap which John politely refused on behalf of them both, excusing himself that he had better ensure that the "lads", in fact, they also employed three stable girls, including Sam, who were always referred to as lads, had secured the yard before they had gone to bed.

They made their way down the gravel drive waving as Patrick and Melanie watched them, although Charlie seemed to have sobered she was still having trouble walking in a straight line and was laughing hysterically at herself and her attempts as she went.

"What a great night, they are lovely", enthused Melanie as they closed the door. "I didn't know that you were so friendly?"
"After I introduced myself that night I've met them a few times in the pub on Quiz Nights, but it's the first time I've ever seen them let their hair down, they are a nice couple, though aren't they?"
"Fancy a nightcap?"
"Yes, I'll share a brandy with you älskling" as Patrick walked towards the drinks cupboard, which was a full unit in the kitchen, he wiped two lead crystal balloons before filling with a very generous measure of his most expensive cognac.

As he turned to hand the balloon to Melanie there was a hammering at the door which startled them both and as he opened the door a shaking and incoherent Charlie stumbled in throwing herself at Patrick and pointing outside.

Melanie gave her a slap across the face to stop her hysterics which seemed to do the trick,
"We've found a body, call the police".
"Where's John?"
"With the, the ......"
"Where?"
"On the way home", she stammered pointing to the end of the driveway.

"OK, Melanie, call the Police, I'll go and find John", giving the large brandy to Charlie, "drink this straight down it'll help".
"I'll be back soon and lock the doors", he called over his shoulder as he ran down the drive.

He caught up with John standing guard over the body which was lying in the ditch at the side of road with the head covered in blood but the eyes staring towards the starry sky, confirming the fact that he was dead.

"Any idea who he is?" Patrick asked.
"I think it's Michael Adams", replied a shaken John as they heard the first of the sirens in the distance away towards Malton.

They stood in silence waiting for the Police to arrive, not feeling the cold.
"Move 20 metres down the road please". ordered the first constable jumping from the L200 illuminated by the flashing blue lights and immediately put up signs to block off the road.

Two other police cars followed in the next couple of minutes, the second manned by Patrick's favourite crime-fighting duo of Crowe and Miller.

Crowe took charge of the scene and did all the right things; checked the scene hadn't been interfered with, made sure the witnesses were OK, instructed officers to tape off the scene and when he saw the body immediately called for a CSI team to gather any forensic evidence.

Maybe he had misjudged him?

"Oh, it's you", he snapped on seeing Patrick, "You the one to find him?"

"No it was my friend here, John"

"Right I need you both to wait in the car while I finish here and I'll have some questions for you"

Luckily, DC Heather Miller sat in the car and began to quiz John about the circumstances in a calm, sympathetic manner, realising that he may well be in shock.

Having collected the few details that John and Patrick could provide, she offered to have them taken home and an officer to visit them tomorrow to take statements.

Patrick thanked her but said they would walk back the couple of hundred yards to Oaktree where Charlie was waiting, being comforted by Melanie.

Charlie had calmed down by the time they arrived, notably with another large brandy in her hand.

"Who was it?" she enquired shakily.

"I think it's Michael Adams", John replied, "but what he would be doing there at his time of night I can't imagine".

"That's if he was killed there? Let the Police do their work and let's not jump to any conclusions, hey?" Patrick exclaimed, "The road will be closed though until tomorrow, so you may as well stay here tonight. Why not call Simon and let him know and he will look after the horses until you're back?"

"I'll make the spare bed up. Do you and John want another Brandy?"
"I'll get them while you see to the bed", Patrick offered.

An hour later, when they had talked about Michael and how he could have possibly been there and interestingly, something that they had forgotten to tell the Police, why the lads hadn't seen him when they walked home after the pub a short time before? The effects of the brandy and the log fire had relaxed them enough to go to bed and hopefully sleep, as Charlie looked very pale and tired.

John and Charlie were collected by Simon just after ten the following morning, as the road was now open, and they gave their statements to DC Miller shortly after arriving home.

"Yes it was Michael Adams", DC Miller told them and "Yes it looks like he was murdered", she went on before asking the routine questions. "Where were you between ten and midnight last night?" which they could answer and others which they couldn't like "Did you see or hear anyone or anything out of the ordinary?".
The only thing that DC Miller found interesting was the fact that the lads had walked past the spot a couple of hours before and no one saw anything, which meant that they had helped with the time of death or more probably narrowed down the timeframe when the body was dumped.

The Police left and they got back to normal running the yard, but with no arrests and no feedback from the Police there was an air of uncertainty in everything that happened in the village for a week or so, as Police cars which were never seen normally became an everyday occurrence.

Everyone had their own suspicions, but most people wisely kept these to themselves.

Chapter 20

With Adams now dead, surely that was the end of the puzzle regarding his strange racing pattern.

After all, it was a good bet that whatever he had been doing and with whom, they would have kept the dealings to themselves, if there *were* illegal activities, which had yet to be proved.

Alexandra Adams had assumed control of the Yard and everyone wondered just how long there would be a racing stable, fully expecting the spendthrift wife to sell to property developers for new housing if they could get planning permission. There had always been rumours of sexual shenanigans with Adam's Head Lad, Seamus Collins, a six-foot, lithe and fit ex-jump jockey who everyone knew to be knowledgeable enough to be a very good trainer but much preferred to make money, however he could and had a known addiction to gambling.

In the meantime, however, Alexandra assured everyone that now she owned the yard, she would be carrying on the business as usual with Seamus as the new trainer-in-waiting.

Thursday's Quiz Night was as busy as usual and during the first break Justin nodded to Patrick and looked towards the rear door indicating that he needed quiet chat outside.

Fully expecting the reason to be his usual reward for a successful tip, he slipped a £20 note for the tip on Devil's Advocate which won at Southwell on Monday at 8/1 and after ensuring no one was around, told Patrick about the plans for the coming week.

He thought it very strange that no one showed any concern for the dead trainer, even though murder was thought to be the inevitable conclusion.

"I can't believe it Chief", whispered Justin looking around cagily, "Next Wednesday we're sending a couple to Marseille for Fridays All-Weather Meeting", meaning the Marseille Pont-de-Vivaux Racecourse with its new Polytrack course, "God knows why, just throwing money away, they've no chance. I thought this madness would end after... well you know"

"Thanks for the tip Justin", Patrick tapped the side of his nose confirming this was confidential.

"You know me Chief, just between us", as Justin tapped the side of his nose.

"He feels like he's just become a Freemason," Patrick thought to himself.

They walked back into the pub separately just as Peter had started Round 2, which this week was on food and drink, and Patrick, spotting John and Charlie, made his way through the crowded bar.

So, whatever was going on looked to be good to be spoiled by a murder.

Later that evening, Patrick looked up the Marseille Racecourse on Google and calculated the cost of the trip, some 990 miles and a 15-hour journey by car, to be over £1000 and with prize money for even the best two races, which Patrick doubted the horses would be running in, given Justin's knowledgeable opinion, was just over £3500, it did seem possible that if one of the two won, they could conceivably make a small profit.

But surely there would be a race closer to home without risking £1000 plus of expenses and he couldn't see any owner wanting to take that gamble. There had to be more to it.

Knowing that Mullins Transport would be transporting the horses meant that it would be very easy to follow them and this time he would not let them out of his sight.

Melanie was not visiting this weekend, she had been asked to cover a programme for John Cross who was recovering from a dose of 'flu, so Patrick decided it was time to confide in Dan and drove over on Sunday lunchtime to meet Dan in his local, The Wheatsheaf Inn in Borrowby, just 100m along the road from the small new housing development of Moors Gardens where Dan and Nanya had a lovely new 4-bedroomed detached.

Over a couple of pints of Daleside Bitter, he relayed the story of his wasted trip to Ireland and what he believed must have happened, although he had to admit it was a wild guess at best.

Dan listened intently as he knew Patrick well enough to know that if he believed that something illegal was happening, he was quite prepared to believe it, regardless of how flimsy the evidence, or indeed lack of it.

Patrick outlined his plan for the following week and whilst it seemed innocuous enough, Dan had a nagging doubt in his mind that if they were going to all this trouble on a regular basis then it had to be worth it. The problem was that they still had no idea exactly what the late Adams was doing (and who was now giving the instructions) and therefore had little idea of the scale of the risk Patrick was taking should he be caught. Was it localised? How many people were involved? Was it Organised Crime? Was it International? Patrick's assertion that he would soon find out only made Dan more uncomfortable.

Again, hiring a car from Enterprise in Malton, the receptionist Kim was now on first name terms, Patrick chose a nondescript metallic Silver Citroen DS4 turbo diesel Automatic, with European Satellite Navigation built-in. With what looked to be sumptuous heated, black leather seating to make the journey as comfortable as possible, he also guessed that a Citroen, especially in a neutral colour, would be unlikely to stand out from the crowd in France.

If he could still use the Police systems to check bookings on Ferry's into and leaving the country, he thought to himself, he would not have to second guess all the time.

Armed with a fresh bag of oranges from Tesco in
Malton, he looked at all the options open to Adams
and Mullins and whilst the Dover to Calais route was
the obvious choice, he was not one hundred percent
convinced.

Although he had guessed the route to Ireland easily
enough, they had still managed to give him the slip
for a couple of hours, even if it was his own stupid
fault and he would need to follow them much more
closely this time and be prepared.

So prepared, that he had purchased a pair of Canon
night-vision binoculars from the local camera shop in
Malton together with a Sony compact camera that did
far more than professional photographers' cameras
did just ten years ago, he would have to try to keep up
with technology he told himself.

Packing for the journey, he also put in a heavy-duty
metal-cased torch, which as well having luminous
halogen bulbs was also gloriously heavy if he needed
to use it to protect himself.

He was just zipping the top of the holdall when his
mobile rang, it was Dan.
"They are booked onto the 3.30pm P&O Dover to
Calais service and back on the 4.30pm return on
Sunday so it's a long trip"
"Thanks for that but why did you bother to check?"
"Well if there is something going on and Melanie or
Nanya found out that I hadn't helped, can you
imagine the grief I'd get. Nayna may only be little but
you seriously don't want to cross her!"
"OK, thanks, mate, see you when I get back and we'll
compare notes".

So, he knows where they were sailing from, but then he was almost certain he knew that they were sailing from Holyhead and still lost them, but they would go along the A64 to join the A1 South, of that much he was sure and he would be waiting for them.

If you have ever questioned your self-will to see through an undertaking, waiting in a freezing cold lay-by in the middle of the night, amidst a line of massive articulated lorries with the cab curtains drawn, the drivers warm, fast asleep and able to wake refreshed for the new day ahead, as you try to stay focussed on the passing traffic with only the through-the-night programmes on Radio 2 for company, then this is the time for wondering just how strong your resolve really is.

Patrick thought of Melanie and the changes in their relationship, the massive change the success of his book had brought about and began to wonder how these two factors would shape his future when he almost missed the familiar maroon and silver transporter flash by the side of his car a good hour before he realistically expected it to and silently patted himself on the back for getting there so early, just in case.

Two hours later it seemed the world was beginning to wake up as the A1 started to grind to a halt just before Peterborough Services, giving him plenty of time to see the Transporter pull into the inside lane before turning right at the top of the slip road, entering the service area and parking up.

Patrick pulled into the Car Park and made an immediate dash straight to the Gents Toilet, he would take every opportunity whenever possible to avail himself of toilets, but otherwise he was completely self-sufficient for the journey with a stash of six, litre sized, screw top bottles of Harrogate Spring Water (they may need to be used for other purposes later on if absolutely necessary) Hob Nob biscuits, Country Grain Cereal Bars, fruit, his indispensable bag of oranges and though he ate very little chocolate, a six-pack of Mars Bars.

This time, he was well prepared, he had learned his lesson.

He had eaten his first Cereal Bar and an Orange before the Transporter pulled back onto the motorway and immediately stopped as the traffic was stationary, with Patrick now refreshed, just six cars behind.

Leaving the A1M, opting to take the A14 towards Cambridge and the A11 to the M25, the traffic was stop-start all the way to Stansted Airport and at one point he wondered whether they would make the ferry, before, as if someone had waved a magic wand, the traffic seemed to disappear on the stroke of 9am and Patrick found himself just three cars behind his quarry and decided he would need to fall back to avoid being noticed.

Pulling into Dover Port at 1pm, he produced his ticket and drove straight through Customs to wait in line a dozen or so vehicles behind the Transporter but three lanes to the left, together with other passenger cars.

With all the vehicles blocked in and going nowhere, Patrick got out and stretched his legs, around the passenger side, out of sight, before visiting the welcomed passenger toilets.

He was washing his hands when the red-haired Mullins walked in, humming to himself as he passed behind Patrick before entering a cubicle at the end of the row.

What was Mullins doing driving his own Transporter instead of the usually hired help?

Did it mean that this was a big event about to happen? He would need to be even more careful as whilst Patrick didn't know Mullins as such, he had been in The Margrave once when Patrick was in with John and Charlie.

He couldn't risk being recognised so hurriedly walked back and quickly glancing across to the Transporter through the Citroen's windows before getting back in, he saw that both the dark, boxer-like Bălan and the flame-haired McLaughlin were both standing outside smoking.

He jumped in and quickly reclined the seat, making sure his head was below the window level.

His mind was racing.

Did Mullins only drive when they smuggling, if that is what they are doing and if so, then why the detour on the way to Holyhead?

That meant that there was a team of three to take two horses?

Maybe he was getting paranoid, it was a thousand-mile trip, of course, they would need to swap drivers, wouldn't they?

But that made the economics even less justifiable with the cost of an extra man for the trip.
His instincts made the hairs on his neck stand up, when this occurred he was seldom wrong, it was like a sixth sense.

The Ferry crossing was just 90 minutes but Patrick made the best of the opportunity to catch up on some sleep and huddled down inside his Barbour, pulling his navy scarf over his ears and the lower half of his face to maintain some degree of anonymity and setting his mobile alarm for one hour, went to sleep. Waking to a buzzing in his chest, he quickly turned off the alarm, and went in search of the gangways to the vehicle decks, he didn't want to lose them now. Passing through one of the crowded bars he caught sight of Mullins and McLaughlin drinking whisky, large ones, not for the first time Bălan was nowhere to be seen.

As the ferry docked and the tannoy invited drivers to return to their vehicles, Patrick joined the hoards as they jostled for position down the stairways. They would all get off in their turn, they were parked in a line, so why the mad rush, just like airline passengers who must take their luggage from the overhead bins before the seatbelt sign has been turned off - their cases are still in the hold for God's sake, Duh!!

Rant over, he turned on the ignition and found that he still had three-quarters of a tank of diesel, good choice for this trip he thought believing that Mullins would have to stop for fuel before he did.

He was glad of the nap and felt fully alert when he followed the Transporter at a distance along the southbound A26, AutoRoute des Anglais passing east of Arras before passing to the west of Reims. The dark winter night made following Mullins much more difficult as if he was close enough to see the vehicle clearly, they may well spot he was following them, but if he dropped too far back he had to concentrate on the red lights on the top, rear edge of the tailgate which would be easy to lose should there be any similar vehicles travelling the same route, he was glad he had taken the opportunity of a nap as he realised that they would be able to share the driving, although two of them had been drinking on the ferry. Did this mean they would be parking up somewhere soon?

Patrick had been so intent on watching the back of the Transporter that he failed to notice the two men in the black Vauxhall Insignia hatchback following a discreet four hundred metres behind.

Mullins Transporter pulled into the Buffalo Grill Autogrill Reims Champagne on the A4, 22kms to the South of Reims. The A4 circles Reims before splitting with the A4 heading east whilst the route to the south again becomes the A26, confusing? Maybe.

He was certainly glad of the Satnav.

Patrick was forced to park behind a dirty, dusty, Beige Renault Espace at the far end of the car park, as this was just visible by the subdued amber glow of the well-lit AutoRoute. Anywhere else and he would have been instantly visible to the Mullins team and having tracked them all this way, this was something that he couldn't afford.

Watching the three leave the truck and head into the restaurant, he realised that he was hungry as well as dog tired but daren't risk closing his eyes in case he missed them like last time, so unwrapping the cheese salad baguette he had bought on leaving the ferry, he ate it whilst staring at the restaurant door. Not the thing to do when you are trying to stay awake but necessary nevertheless.

Forty minutes later the trio returned to the Transporter and having checked the horses, returned to the cab. Patrick prayed that they too would be taking a rest before continuing and was grateful to see the cab lights turned off and the engine still and quiet.

Believing that he could afford to risk at least a few hours he set his mobile phone alarm for 3am, four hours away and zipping himself into his sleeping bag was fast asleep in minutes.

Knowing he had only allowed himself four hours he was awake ten minutes before having dreamed of Melanie as a teenager and taking her fishing for trout whilst wearing just a pair of waders, why couldn't he always have dreams like this?

He was relieved to see the Transporter was still there as he ate a couple of HobNobs washed down with his Harrogate Spring Water.

He must be learning about his targets as at 3am, the diesel engine spluttered into life and almost before Patrick had folded his sleeping bag and stashed it behind the passenger seat, Mullins pulled out onto the southbound A4.

Entering the carriageway behind them, the traffic was much lighter than before and Patrick had to stay at least 600m behind to avoid being conspicuous.

The racecourse at Marseille Pont-de-Vivaux was just south of the A50 and 22kms east of Marseille itself.

Marseille is France's second largest city, on the Mediterranean coast and the largest port for commerce, freight and cruise ships and with a population of just under one million people, the racecourse attracts large crowds. This would make tracking the three of them difficult even if they stayed together, if they split up it would be impossible, so Patrick had to put together a plan based on the most likely scenario.

He still wondered why Mullins himself was on the trip instead of just his drivers but why was it necessary to take horses if it wasn't a betting scam and both John and Justin assured him wasn't?

The only logical explanation was that if it wasn't the horses and it wasn't just something personal, otherwise, why the need to take the horses, then it had to involve the Transporter. Patrick convinced himself that this had to be the reason and vowed not to leave the truck, regardless of what Mullins's crew did.

The racecourse had parking for five hundred and twenty cars and even at 10am on the day of the December meeting, in cold, windy and dismal conditions, the car park was busy with corporate customers using the many meeting rooms and seminars at the course and Patrick managed to park in Row 8 at the western end of the car park in clear sight of the commercial vehicle park with its collection of horseboxes. He watched as Bălan and McLaughlin unloaded the horses and walked them to the stable block before returning to the truck.

He didn't understand the significance of the navy-blue transporter belonging to Henri Duvall Racing which had pulled alongside Mullins, but having missed the opportunity to find out what their extra-curricular business entailed, he resigned himself to a long watching brief.

Managing to use the Racecourse facilities throughout the day and supplementing his diet of fruit and biscuits with a cheeseburger and fries, as this was France, even the junk food tasted good, he scarcely missed a minute away from watching the transporter in the now quiet vehicle park.

The car park continued to fill up and the day was so dark that the lights on the course, in the entrances and the reception area shone as if it was a night meeting.

As the afternoon meeting started the stadium was almost full, no small achievement with Christmas just a couple of weeks away, and the sound of the public-address system struggled to be heard over the boisterous crowd who appeared to be getting into the holiday mood early.

Although Mullins and his drivers were nowhere to be seen, Patrick stuck to his plan of watching the Transporter as, with the size of the crowd, he would be just as likely to be spotted by Mullins as a familiar face as he would be to keep a close watch on Mullins.

Peeling yet another orange, he saw Bălan saunter languidly through the lines of vehicles back to the truck, followed a few metres behind by a tall, dark-haired man of indeterminate age but his first thought was that he was too well dressed to be just a driver.

As Bălan stood outside his cab, looking around anxiously, the other person jumped athletically up into the cab of the Henri Duvall Racing Transporter.

Patrick sensed that something was about to happen and took out his Canon Compact Camera which also had a video record facility and focussed it just in time to see Bălan pull a pistol from under his jacket and open the cab door.

Simultaneously the cab door of the French truck opened and four Oriental looking girls were forced to climb down from the French truck and up into the cab of Mullins Transporter.

Bălan handed a khaki coloured duffel bag to the other driver before climbing into the cab and closing the door whilst the other driver climbed in and closed the door of the dark blue Henri Duvall truck.

Everything now began to fall into place in Patrick's mind. The reason for the uneconomic trips was not to transport horses to the races but to bring back people, whether illegal immigrants or even worse, judging by what he just witnessed, sex-slaves and very young at that.

Patrick played back the recording on the small rear screen of the camera, unsure of the quality of any recording he may have made, and realised from the playback timer that the whole operation had taken just ninety seconds from Bălan opening the cab door to closing it again. The quality of the recording was excellent. Be thankful for technology he told himself as he thought of the effect this recording would have in court for this was surely a monumental piece of evidence and fully vindicated Patrick's instinct to follow Mullins.

With the Transporter parked in a tight line and unable to leave until the three trucks in front moved and with Mullins and McLaughlin still absent, Patrick carefully made his way into the racecourse building, used the facilities, bought food for the journey home at the bar, if indeed they were headed home, and called Dan on his mobile.

"Patrick, where are you?"

"I'm in Marseille and listen I need to be quick. They are smuggling people, they have 4 young Oriental girls, maybe illegals, maybe sex workers, but they will probably be coming through Dover tomorrow evening. See what you can organise. Got to go", and with that ended the call as he sighted the red hair of McLaughlin following Mullins out of the grandstand and wasn't prepared to lose them having come this far.

Chapter 21

Stella always knew in her heart that this day would come, ever since Stuart had got himself involved with the Family.

One thing that she had always been taught by her family in Ireland however, was to always look after yourself, and not just physically, although she was as strong as any man and from her upbringing as the only girl in the family with seven older brothers, she could fight like a banshee if the need arose, as Michael Adams had found out to his cost in the bedroom of The Grouse and Hare some months ago.

Poor Michael, it had been good whilst it lasted, but was it her fault that he had fallen for her? True, he had told her that he had never had a woman like her before but should she have broken it off earlier before he got too deeply involved?
Maybe, but at the time she had to admit to herself that she enjoyed the excitement, the danger, the sex as much as he did and it wasn't as if they had not agreed at the outset that it was just no strings attached fun, was it? No, it was sad, but she didn't feel that she was to blame.

Adams had not learned however, despite the bruises forcing him to wear Polo neck sweaters for over a week and although she had not seen him since, he had persisted with ringing her and had tried his hardest to both persuade or occasionally even threaten her until she stopped answering the phone, he must have been in love her, she mused.

She had not learned either in that respect, as she had turned to Stefan Bălan to keep her sexual appetite sated, using the flat over the garage whenever possible and the back of her Mercedes when there were too many people around the yard.

It was, she thought, a good swap, the younger, fitter and more muscular Bălan for the older, slightly overweight Adams.

She thought it only a matter of time before he would have confronted Mullins with the truth and not only would this break her naïve husband's heart, she knew from experience that he had a wicked temper.
On one occasion, early in their relationship, when he had caught her flirting with another man she had been on the wrong end of a beating and this was something she wished to avoid at all costs, for both their sakes, as she was a lot stronger person now and if would be touch and go who won any fight.

But Michael was gone, and with him went the potential problem.

Her father had told her many, many times to always make sure that you had money. If you had money you could go anywhere, do anything and be anyone and this was advice she had always embraced.

The advice had made her take good care of her future security so the time was right therefore for her own sake as well as that of Stuart, for her to disappear and start a new life, somewhere warm and safe.

She knew Stuart would be OK.

He could continue to earn enough money from the Mafia business and just get a girl in to help do the transport bookings, couldn't he?
Bălan could continue to run the smuggling operations for the Family, for Mullins had made her believe they were bringing in drugs and firearms, not people.
She would have had nothing to do with people trafficking.

It was useful that she had always overseen the business accounts and since the involvement with the Rumanians and the large amounts of cash coming in, Mullins had been so focussed on this that he had completely taken his eye off the ball with the legitimate side of the business. This provided her with the opportunity to empty the business accounts of just over fifty-seven thousand pounds into her Bank of Ireland account, that she had held in the name of Stella Dooley since she was fifteen years old.
She had never closed the account which her husband knew nothing about, keeping it in her maiden name and, following her father's advice, she had over the years diverted money from the Transport business and a few investments of her own and, unbeknown to Stuart, it already contained over ninety-thousand pounds. When she left, she would need to transfer this quickly to a new account in a different name and had learned all about ways to transfer monies from account to account in different countries to avoid any chance of it being traced.

One good thing about dealing with the Mafia and sleeping with Bălan was that he could supply her with a fake passport, which he did without question in the name of Marian Doherty, just in case she needed to get away quickly if they were caught by the police. With this she could walk into the travel agents in Malton and book a ten-day Christmas and New Year break to Marbella, flying from Newcastle to Alicante in Spain, but with no intention of returning.

Before she left she also helped herself to the thirty odd thousand pounds in cash that had been stashed in the array of brown envelopes in the sideboard that Stuart had carelessly not invested or hidden securely and the fifteen thousand that she had hidden around the house and office in smaller amounts since that first operation.

She knew that the time was right, her husband and sex-partner Bălan were both in France. It had to be now and with the new identity and with money, she could disappear without a trace.

She packed a single, old, large brown suitcase, carefully concealing the money in the middle of her clothes.

Taking a taxi to the railway station, she left no note. She decided that it would be best if she gave no reasons for going, that way everyone could make up their own minds, she may even have been kidnapped she thought to herself as, with her Mercedes parked forlornly on the driveway, she left without looking back.

Her dad had told her she could go anywhere, do anything and be anybody and she would do just that.

Check-in at the airport was her first moment of anxiety as she lifted the case onto the waiting conveyor belt under the gaze of the check-in clerk. "Did you pack the case yourself?" she heard the clerk ask and realised that the case containing over fifty-thousand pounds and with it her new life was disappearing and going through the airport checks, what if they found the cash? How would she account for it? Why had she not considered this before and just driven abroad, she could have bought a car for a few thousand and no one would have known, she began to feel very stupid.

Walking towards the airport passport control she almost had a panic attack. How good was the forgery? It looked OK to her, but what about the security staff who knew what to look for? She hoped and prayed that the Family was as good as they claimed.

Walking straight through and emptying her bag with just keys and a purse, she walked through the security x-ray when it beeped and the two attendants, one male, and one female, told her to stop. They asked her to remove her earrings and watch and walk through again.

No beep! She was so stressed she had almost wet herself.

Still with an hour before boarding, she dropped the keys from her bag into a waste bin.

She wouldn't be needing those again, and it felt like another tie with her old life was being cut as she bought a coffee from the Costa Coffee stall and sat counting off the minutes, watching airport security and trying not to look guilty, hoping they had not discovered the cash in the suitcase.

If the flight was on time, Stuart would not be home when she landed in Spain and she wondered just what he would do when he returned and found her gone. "Would he be more upset at losing her or the money?" she mused.
What about Stefan? She would miss the excitement, but where she was going there would be plenty of men. Young, fit men and with money to dress well was sure that she would not be short of attention. Maybe with her new identity, she could even land herself a millionaire?

She was still attractive, Michael and Bălan had both confirmed that as they had done all the chasing, not her.
She had worked hard all her life, wasn't it time for someone to spoil her now?

She slept uncomfortably on the plane, with two young children on the row directly behind her alternately either crying and screaming or fighting and kicking each other, how pleased she was at this minute that they had not had any children, she couldn't stand kids nowadays!

The plane landed without incident at Alicante just fifteen minutes late and having cleared Passport Control she virtually sprinted to Baggage Carousel 3 to retrieve her bag. The bags were not yet coming through and she watched impatiently as the metal and rubber carousel containing a shoe, a teddy bear and a battered holdall from previous flights circled unloved and unclaimed.

The first cases appeared and the passengers crammed the space between the yellow line, put there to help all passengers see their bags as they dropped onto the conveyor, and the belt itself, forcing people to push into every available space and had no room to manoeuvre their cases when they did manage to grab them from the slowly moving belt.

Stella's anxiety increased with every batch of cases that appeared and were collected by fellow passengers who with filled luggage trolleys made their way to the coaches that were waiting to take the holidaymakers to their hotels, which were parked in long rows outside the busy airport.

After what seemed to be an eternity, actually just seven minutes, the battered case, still intact, appeared and she pulled it gratefully through the crowd and made her way out into the pleasant, afternoon sunshine and her new life.

Chapter 22

Patrick's biggest problem on the journey north on the A26 was staying awake.

The Transporter drivers were obviously taking turns at the wheel and stopped only for fuel and what looked like a massive Burger King takeaway, in four bulging large brown paper bags displaying the famous logo, south of Reims, giving Patrick time to refill the Citroen, which he did facing the car and hiding his face from view for fear of being recognised and stock up on bottled water and a crusty, freshly-made ham and cheese baton.

The journey was long and uneventful. their speed was steady, always slightly below the speed limit, and even though the traffic thinned out through the dark, frosty night, Patrick was mindful to keep well back, at times giving them up to 800m on the straight sections. Thank goodness it's not foggy, he thought to himself.

Approaching Arras, 110 kilometres south of Calais, Patrick called Dan.
"Hi this is Dan, please leave a message," followed by a long, continuous beep was the response.
"Dan it's Patrick, call me when you get the message please"

Fifteen minutes later he tried again with the same result, he needed to know if Dan had alerted the British Police as once they entered the UK, anything could happen.

If he lost them at the port, they could be destined for anywhere in the country and catching them would be challenging if not impossible.

Surely Dan would have acted?

A further 10 minutes passed and he tried again, no answer. Where was he?

The port came into sight and he followed Mullins, a dozen or so vehicles behind, into the queue for the 4.30pm P&O Sailing to Dover.

"Dan I need you to call me now and tell me what's happening, I'm about to board the Ferry." He hated leaving voicemails but needs must he told himself.

Once the vehicles were loaded, Patrick watched Mullins, McLaughlin and Bălan make their way to the bar whilst he went on deck figuring that if Dan called, he could at least take the call and find somewhere quieter to speak. Following overnight gales along the south coast, the crossing was rough and there were more than a few passengers who were parting with their lunches over the side, ground baiting his dad being a coarse fisherman used to call it, though the affected passengers would certainly not have seen the funny side at this moment.

As they approached the Port of Dover, Patrick was still no wiser as to whether Dan had relayed the information to the Kent Police, Customs & Excise, Immigration or anyone else and he had no idea what he was supposed to do when they disembarked.

Follow at a distance? Alert the Port Authorities? Call 999? If so, did he do it after they entered the country or whilst they were still on the Ferry? His mind raced but reached no acceptable conclusion.

The Ferry docked and the claxon sounded for drivers to return to their vehicles as the ramp was lowered and the ferry doors opened, the sickly smell of diesel and oil that filled the vehicle decks now beginning to disperse as the gusts of sea air quickly forced its way into the ferry.

The vehicles formed an orderly queue to leave the area through the Customs barriers, very British he thought with his mind temporarily distracted.

Patrick could see the Maroon and Silver livery of the Transporter in the line to the right of his Citroen making its way slowly to the raised barrier as suddenly all hell broke loose.

A black Vauxhall Insignia broke out of the line with sirens wailing and blue lights flashing as it forced its way through the queues towards the barrier, with the lines of traffic moving to make way to let it through. The barrier crashed down to a cacophony of car horns and the blaring deep-throated roars of HGV air horns as the Insignia closed on the Transporter.

Cab doors were flung open and Mullins fell out of the passenger side as the fit and muscular Bălan and the lithe, flame-haired Mclaughlin jumped from the driver's side and raced along the quayside, hotly pursued by two armed officers who had abandoned the unmarked Vauxhall, creating mayhem for the ferry passengers who were still intent on leaving the docks and heading home.

With Bălan and McLaughlin being pursued, Patrick sprang from the Citroen and hurdled the bonnet of a yellow, French registered Renault Clio to much shouting and fist waving from the elderly occupants. He caught Mullins. Aware that he would not outrun the police, attempting to hide beneath a container lorry that was waiting to board the next ferry to leave for France and took great pleasure in dragging him from his impromptu hideaway before pinning him to the ground with his hands behind his back.
"You are not obliged to say anything.........." he started out of habit before realising that he no longer had the DI rank or even a Warrant Card, let alone handcuffs.

Fortunately, two uniformed police came to his assistance.
"Patrick Spencer?"
"Yes, how did you ..." before he could complete the sentence he saw Dan running towards him.
"Sorry I couldn't call you back but I didn't want to spoil the surprise", he grinned as shots rang out from further along the quayside and everyone instinctively took cover.

"There are four girls in Mullins' Transporter somewhere, help me get them out Dan", as he ran towards the now vacated truck with Mullins now arrested and being led away to the waiting Police Range Rover.

Obviously the girls had heard the sirens and the gunshots and it was possible to hear their muffled screams as the pair approached.

"Be careful Patrick", Dan called out, "it may be booby trapped", but Patrick had waited a long time to be part of an operation again and bounded up the step into the cab, shouting "Police" as loud as he could. He reckoned that whatever nationality the young girls were, they would understand the word Police and hopefully begin to realise that they were safe.

Along the quayside, surrounded by four uniformed officers in flak jackets and the two in plain clothes who had leapt from the Insignia, McLaughlin lay prostrate, handcuffed, bleeding from a leg wound but alive and waiting for the Paramedics, who were the first medical team on the scene, to determine if he was fit to be moved to the first of the waiting ambulances

Bălan lay 2 metres away with 4 shots to the chest, his eyes staring to heaven, although it was an unlikely destination given his past record. Covering him would be the job of the white-suited CSI team when they arrived and had completed all their mandatory investigations as the Independent Police Complaints Commission would conduct a full enquiry into the shooting to consider whether the officers were justified in shooting the victim.

After following the screams, Patrick and Dan together with WPC Jane Bryan of Kent Constabulary tried to find how the girls had been concealed in the cab as Patrick showed then the video of Bălan forcing the girls into the truck at gunpoint.

Removing the sleeper cab bed, Dan found the clips that allowed the back panel to be removed and pulling it down revealed the four terrified young girls, all clinging together, one of them refusing to open her eyes as if that would somehow protect her.
On seeing the WPC in uniform the youngest flung herself hysterically at Jane and clung on as if her life depended on it, refusing to believe that their ordeal was over.

McLaughlin was taken under Police guard to Buckland Hospital on Coombe Valley Road in Dover where he underwent minor surgery to remove a bullet from his thigh but when he came around from the operation, refused to say anything to the Police, claiming that if he did they would find a way to get to him and he was a dead man. He gave no indication of who "they" were and refused to speak any further.

Mullins however claimed that he was forced to carry out his part in the operations as they, this time naming the Rumanian Mafia, had threatened to kill Stella if he did not work for them and he blamed them for Adams' murder as Adams' had demanded a larger slice of the profits if he were to continue providing horses for the bogus operations.

He believed Bălan was the one who had killed Adams and this would add credence to his story of intimidation as Bălan was, if they believed him, a murderous thug living on the premises and therefore in an ideal position to threaten Stella.

After being checked out medically, the girls were all physically fit even if they would bear the mental scars of their ordeal for a lifetime, they gave their matching accounts to the police interviewers.
The Police interviewers were all experienced female detectives as they continued to nurture the girls' trust as they shied away from all contact with male officers.

They were all Thai and from the Bangkok region. Three of the girls had been abducted, bound and held in a warehouse at the docks before being put into the hold of a cargo ship bound for Marseille. The other had been "sold" by her family.
This revelation had forced a break in the interview by twenty-six-year-old DS Amanda Hampshire, who found it so hard to comprehend that she had had to take ten minutes to walk in the fresh air to compose herself before continuing to extract the full horror of the young girls' experience and wondering how she could ever lead any kind of normal life again having been sold by her family as some kind of commodity!

She knew she would face some horrors when joining the Police but this was just, well, incomprehensible.

They were worse than animals.

Chapter 23

Having satisfied himself that Anne-Marie was safe and her whereabouts were, to the best of his knowledge still secret, the name change on her marriage would make tracing her difficult, although he had to confess, not impossible, he felt that he was now able to carry out the rest of Pavel's instructions.

The chance to work and to help an old friend at the same time gave Josef a feeling of worth that he had not experienced for some time, certainly, since he lost his beloved Elsa and with an unaccustomed smile on his face he picked up the phone and dialled the +44 number.
"This is South Yorkshire Police, press 1 to report a new crime, 2 for traffic, 3 for CID or 4 for all other departments". Very impersonal however, that was the way of the world but Josef didn't approve, he would always prefer to deal with people. as he pressed option 4 a little too late "I'm sorry please press 1 to report a crime, 2 for traffic - Josef pressed 4 again and waited, and waited, eventually a real person answered, there was a God, "South Yorkshire Police, how can I help?"
"Good morning, can I speak with DS Wakefield, please? My name is Josef Weissman, I am an Attorney at Law in Vienna and I assure you that he will wish to speak to me".
"One moment Mr. Weissman, I'll see if he is in".
After only a short interlude with the obligatory music, he was put through.

"Mr. Weissman, DS Wakefield, thank you for calling back, my boss would be very interested if you could tell us anything you know about your Pavel Popescu. I take it you are able to tell us what you know now?"

"Yes DS Wakefield, but you must understand that I needed to make sure that certain people were safe and their whereabouts secret before I put their lives in danger. This may take some time and I have some very specific instructions that I am afraid I must follow".

"That's fine Mr. Weissman, I am going to put the call on speakerphone if that's OK as the team will hear your information direct from the horse's mouth as it were?"

"That is fine DS Wakefield. Pavel knew that he would be a target for the Rumanian Mafia for whom he worked as an accountant. He was persuaded to join them whilst in Doftana prison in Bucharest to enable his early release and the cessation of the daily routine of torture and humiliation. He knew that one day he would be able to find the courage and the opportunity to right the wrongs in which he was forced to become involved."

"Are we talking about murder Mr. Weissman?"

"Please be patient DS Wakefield. Having made his decision to right these wrongs, he was aware that the odds of him being able to disappear were not good and if caught then he knew that they would show no mercy.

It was important to him however that his family, his wife divorced him when he was in prison, but he has a daughter and both a granddaughter and grandson, who he has never seen, and now never will, but they all believed that he was dead. My instructions were to ensure that his family were all safe before I could hand over the book to the Police"

"Book, what book?"

"I have in my possession a large book, a ledger, which details the numbered Swiss Bank Accounts and the transactions carried out on behalf the Rumanian Mafia over a period of almost 20 years. This involves drugs smuggling, arms and people trafficking and will be enough I believe to effectively close a large portion, if not all their operations, across Europe anyway, and put many high-ranking members behind bars. So, you see, although Pavel was forced to do some very bad things, he assured me he was never personally involved in the operations, just the money side of the business, he has tried to make amends and he has paid for it with his life".

"Mr. Weissman, this is DI Bradshaw, you say you have the book, is it with you now?"

"I may be old but I am not foolish DI Bradshaw. The book is safely stored in the vault of the bank that I gave details to DS Wakefield about when we last spoke".

"I would ask that you do nothing until we get there Mr. Weissman, we will be on the next plane. We will call you when we arrive and arrange to meet and please, whatever your instructions, do not contact anyone else".

"I think that would be wise. I will await your call", said a relieved Josef as he hung up.

"Right Wakefield, you better come with me, we need to run this by the Chief Super".

The Chief Super, in fact, Chief Superintendent Alan Lane, a no-nonsense Geordie who had an enviable reputation for being strict but fair and was as quick to praise officers as condemning them and as with all good bosses, the praise was public and the bollockings were in private.

His P.A. Donna knocked and entered.

"DI Bradshaw and DS Wakefield to see you sir and they stress that its most important and urgent that they speak with you and only you".

"OK, send them in", he was intrigued.

"Top Secret, urgent and important hey, I trust you know what you're doing going over people's heads?" Lane spoke without looking up from his desk, "well sit down then and don't look so worried".

"Thank you sir,", they said in unison before Bradshaw asked Wakefield to relay the story.

"Think it's legit, not just some old crank?"

"I checked the name sir and he is registered as an Attorney in Vienna and he seemed to know an awful lot about our body and why he would have been executed, so yes sir I think it's legit".

"Bradshaw?"

"Yes sir, I agree, I believe him".

"OK, so we have the potential to put the major players of the Rumanian Mafia behind bars, solve at least one of our two murders and stop a raft of organised crime in the UK. Does that sum it up?"

"Yes sir", again Bradshaw and Wakefield were like a double act.

"What's your plan then? How can we do it without any cock-ups and make sure we all get the brownie points?"

"Well, sir, firstly I think we are the only ones who know where the book is and therefore we are in prime position to retrieve it. Once we have it back here we can start to verify the contents and work with the forces who need to be involved without losing control and make sure the book never leaves the premises. I would like to take DS Wakefield sir and meet with Mr Weissman in Vienna to bring it back. If it is kept within these walls, no one will know where we are until we are back with it whereas if we create a big operation, who knows who we will end up dealing with and whose side they are on".

"Right", Lane paused with his hands flat on the desk in front of him as he reached a decision. "OK, the only thing I insist on is that you are to be shadowed at all times by two armed, National Crime Agency officers. Come back in five minutes and I will have everything sorted".

Bradshaw and Wakefield left the office both excited about the scale of the case and the potential for international recognition and the effect that this could have on their reputation and careers, and anxious, as it was way above the scale of their normal daily brief, catching local criminals.

A few minutes later Donna called down to the office. "The Chief Superintendent is ready for you now", prompting Bradshaw and Wakefield to drop everything and leave their coffees, which were still hot, on the desk.

"Right this is what will happen. The helicopter will take you both to Stansted where you will meet a DI Mitchell and DS Jones from the NCA before you fly to Vienna.

They will be armed so if you are compromised, get the hell out of there and leave it to the professionals, understand? I don't want any cock-ups. You have an hour to be back here with your bags and anything else you need."

When Wakefield returned, and screeched to a halt in the car park, the helicopter was on the helipad with the rotors turning and Bradshaw was already strapped into the rear seat, wearing Aviation Headsets, or "Cans" as are they are affectionately known, to enable the pilot to speak to his passengers and to block out the noise, protecting the occupants' ears.

No sooner was Wakefield strapped in and with his headset on, the navy blue and yellow liveried helicopter emblazoned with the POLICE lettering lifted off and swung south from Sheffield for the fifty-five minutes' flight.

The flight was bumpy, cold and noisy and for a lot of the time was like being wrapped in a blanket as the low clouds were dense and dark and it was with a great deal of relief on the part of both officers that they touched down at the far end of the airport where the two NCA officers were waiting.

In almost matching leather blouson jackets and faded denim jeans, Mitchell and Jones could have been straight out of a seventies TV Police drama.

Introducing themselves it was evident that whilst Mitchell, who had close-cropped fair hair was undoubtedly a Londoner, the black, wavy-haired Jones possessed a strong Welsh accent and could have come straight from the Welsh Valleys.

The blue lights of the airport security car took them straight to the waiting Eurowings Airbus A319 where they were shown straight to seats on Row 25, the back row, next to the toilets.

The previously green-faced Wakefield, who was now getting some colour back into his cheeks, moaned that wherever their seats where it would be better than the Police Helicopter, bringing a smile to the faces of the other three.

The flight, however, was not full and Rows 23 and 24 was empty, the check-in staff having filled the plane from the front.

The loading seemed to take forever with noisy parties, predominately female, flying off to visit the Vienna Christmas Markets amid a smattering of business people, either travelling to or returning from business meetings and easily identified by their briefcases and iPads and seeking a couple of hours of peace and quiet, which appeared to be wishful thinking.

Taking off in the grey, depressing afternoon, it had never got light today, they were soon above the clouds and the bright sunlight seemed to transform everyone's mood and the groups, who were already in the Christmas spirit ably assisted by the generous measures of Bombay Sapphire and a mere dash of Schweppes Tonic, got noticeably louder.

This, together with the empty rows in front of them, gave the officers a chance to discuss the operation and the plans when they arrived in Vienna without fear of being overheard.

The NCA officers would stay behind Bradshaw and Wakefield, whilst keeping them in sight so that they could keep watch over a much wider radius. yet close enough to be able to protect them both and the book should this be necessary.

It had been agreed that although the NCA Officers would be armed, only Landespolizei-Direktor Hans Heideck, State Commissioner of the Federal Police of Austria in Vienna, knew of the operation but would have officers in waiting should their intervention become necessary. He also gave his permission that although violating Protocol, the two English policemen could enter and carry their weapons in his city.

The operation had to be swift and secret as it was unclear at this point just how far the influence of the Rumanian Mafia stretched and with the potential results contained within the book, no one was taking any chances.

Having cleared the airport security with the help of Heideck, Bradshaw called Weissman.

"We are here Mr. Weissman, is everything OK?"

"Yes DI Bradshaw, everything is OK.".

"Where can we meet?".

"I am keen to hand over the book as soon as possible to fulfil my obligation to Pavel, so why don't you come straight to the Bank. DS Wakefield has the address; I'll meet you there?"

"We are on our way, see you there".

"OK, we are to go straight to the bank, which bank is it?" Bradshaw asked.
"It's the Liechtensteinische Landesbank (Osterreich) AG in Wipplingerstrasse," replied Wakefield reading from his notebook.

With that, they stepped out into the icy cold, snow covered Vienna afternoon and hailed two taxis. Bradshaw gave the address to the first driver and Jones was tempted to say "follow that car" but resisted as Bradshaw also gave the address to the second taxi before the two pulled out in the busy city traffic, full of Christmas shoppers.
The crowds would at least make the officers difficult to target if the Rumanians were following them but more difficult to stay close to the pair as shoppers were jostling along the length and breadth of the pavements, still, the experienced officers had seen no indications of trouble, so far so good.

The taxis arrived at the Bank and Wakefield spotted an old man wrapped up in a dark blue, calf length overcoat with a multi-coloured scarf pulled up around the lower half of his face and wearing an old black fedora, looking around as if waiting for someone.
"Mr. Weissman?" called Wakefield and Josef immediately recognised the voice and reached out to shake hands.
"DS Wakefield, you are here then?" and managed to raise a smile as he realised that of course he was here, it must be the nerves showing his senile side.
"This is DI Bradshaw; shall we go inside?"

Josef insisted on checking the passports of his visitors before entering the bank, where they waited behind an old lady of indeterminate age, dripping in gold and pearl jewellery and wearing many layers of thick woollen clothing atop fur lined boots, who wanted access to her safety deposit box.

"Yes sir, how can I help you?" came from a severe looking but surprisingly cheerful bank clerk in an immaculate charcoal suit, white shirt, and conservative blue tie.

"I would like to retrieve my Safety Deposit Box, number VF 2376742"

"And your name sir?"

"Weissman, Josef Weissman" he replied as he put his passport under the security glass screen.

Having studied the passport and checked the likeness which was still obviously Josef despite the toll of the past 5 years.

"And your password sir?"

Josef wrote the password on a piece of Bank notepaper and passed it under the security screen. "This way sir".

The efficient clerk walked away and opened the security door to Josef's right and he disappeared inside.

All four officers were inside the bank keeping a diligent watch on all the comings and goings and apart from one man dressed in a long, black trenchcoat with an upturned collar who seemed reluctant to show his face, everything appeared normal.

After what seemed to be a half-hour but was in fact just five minutes, Josef returned clutching a package wrapped loosely in plain brown paper and bound with dark-brown string.

Passing this to Bradshaw, he said with a tear in his eye, "take good care of this DI Bradshaw, this is what Pavel gave his life for and hoped this would make amends. Many people will be brought to justice and others will be freed. It is in your hands now; this part of my task is finished. God bless you all", and walked out of the bank as Bradshaw put the package into her holdall and along with Wakefield and the two NCA bodyguards, followed Weissman out of the bank. They were in time to see Josef take a taxi before hailing one themselves.

"Airport please", they called as they climbed into the back of the bright green cab which was advertising a German brand of toothpaste on the side and were joined by Mitchell and Jones.

"Too many people around to try to follow", a nervous Mitchell explained as Jones remained silent, looking through all the windows as though he expected trouble and seeing the black trenchcoated man from the bank climb into a dark blue hatchback which was parked with engine idling a few metres along the street.

"We may have company," Jones said as he unbuttoned the shoulder holster as Mitchell instinctively did the same.

At the second intersection, a white van pulled out straight across the front of the taxi and stopped, forcing the driver to brake hard.

Stopping just before running into the side of the van, two armed men jumped out of the back as the driver was forced to get out of the passenger side as the taxi blocked the driver's door.

"Was zum Teufel.." (What the hell) the taxi driver screamed as Mitchell and Jones drew their guns to open fire.

Shots rang out before they could fire themselves and the would be assailants fell to the ground as one.

Looking around they saw that the dark blue hatchback had pulled up close behind and all four doors were open, four armed men were showing their ID "Police, Police, do not shoot", as the man from the bank walked towards the taxi with his hand still holding his gun, but now raised in the air and his left hand brandishing his Police ID card.

"Willkommen to Vienna DI Mitchell, I am Inspector Josef Eder of the Austrian Police, the Commissioner sends his compliments", he smiled as sirens began to wail in the distance", and has asked that we escort you to the Airport".

The taxi driver looked in no state to drive as he was shaking like a leaf and muttering prayers in German as he played with a string of Rosary Beads, so Eder moved him to the passenger seat and drove the cab, closely followed by the blue hatchback back to Vienna International Airport some 18 km southeast of central Vienna and left the local police, who had arrived within minutes, to clear up the bodies and the mess they left behind.

Back on the plane, the officers were still in a high state of alert and found it hard to sit still, every move in front of them being a potential threat.
They had already spoken to their counterparts in the UK and requested armed protection on their arrival and the presence was apparent as soon as they disembarked via the back exit of the Airbus and whisked away to the waiting helicopter.

Saying their goodbyes to Mitchell and Jones, Bradshaw and Wakefield jumped aboard the helicopter which was surrounded by police cars with blue flashing lights and were airborne in seconds, the book safely stored in Bradshaw's holdall.

"If that's what they will do to get at it, there must be some very revealing information in here," as Bradshaw patted her bag, not realising just how revealing.

Chapter 24

The book took forty-eight hours to give up its secrets regarding the operations in the UK and yielded not only the financial details of the Mafia's finances which would be frozen globally but details of hundreds of operations throughout Europe including drugs, arms, and people trafficking for the sex industry.

Chief Constables from across the country were informed and at ten o'clock on Thursday evening a secure conference call was made involving all Chief Constables, ACC and Media Officers with the DCIs who would undertake responsibility for the morning's operations for which they were promised unlimited support and resources. This was too big an opportunity to fail.

At 6am, armed police in marked high-speed cars and Transit Vans gathered outside Veronica's in Sheffield and all other branches of Veronica's in the North as well as a chain of Massage Parlours branded as Hedonism across the West Midlands.

Their brief was simple.

Arrest everyone inside and stop them making any phone calls; at all costs.

At Veronica's in Sheffield, the place was in darkness, the last customers having left around 3am and the girls, locked in their dark, damp rooms had only just gone to bed having entertained up to twenty men during their shift.

Specialist Firearms Officer (SFO) Sean Dugdale waited in the Transit awaiting the order from the officer-in-charge, DCI Will Smith to enter the premises. Whilst waiting he quickly worked out the figures, ten girls, £100 a time, fifteen customers each, £15,000 a night, 7 nights a week that's £105,000 a week. No wonder organised gangs saw prostitution as a goldmine and could afford to grease a few palms to obtain planning permission for these brothels.

The radio crackled into life.

Ready team 1, Sir, Ready team 2, Sir, Ready team 3, Sir - Go Go Go was the order as the officers scrambled from the squad cars to follow the three SFOs and the officer with the Enforcer, the Police battering Ram which enabled officers to gain access to locked premises in seconds with a minimum of resistance.
"Police lay down your weapons and lie on the floor", was the shout as the door frame splintered under the three tonnes of impact force from the battering ram as the door flew inwards allowing the SFOs to enter the building and neutralise any resistance they encountered.
They moved through the dark, lurid black and pink decorated reception area.

Shouting "clear", they moved into the main theatre, with a long white-metal shuttered bar, three floor-to-ceiling poles on carpeted podiums and large, wall-mounted, widescreen TVs which were used to show erotic films to get the customers in the mood to be entertained.

"Clear" came the shout as the three used their rifle mounted lights to scan the area, as two shots rang out from the rear of the premises.

"Dugdale, rear entrance" shouted Smith and Dugdale, with his weapon held at shoulder height and the steel rifle butt tight into his right shoulder, immediately walked towards the corridor leading to the toilets and the rear door which was open.

"Officer Down", he shouted into his lapel-mounted radio as he saw a uniformed officer lying at the foot of the two cold, stone steps leading to the rear brick-paved courtyard, filled with overflowing refuse bins. He walked through the rear door, gun poised ready to return fire, but the area was clear.

"Yard Clear", he called as he heard a noise behind him immediately followed by the loud retort of a Police Heckler & Koch MP5SF.

Turning around he saw the body of a shaven headed gunman in tracksuit bottoms and trainers with a heavyweight fleece fall to the ground fatally wounded.

SFO Mark Turner was standing with his gun pointing at the body to ensure there was no chance of a reply as he kicked away a Glock pistol belonging to the floored doorman before opening the toilet doors and searching for any other would be assailants.

"Clear", he shouted into his radio, the corridor filling with officers coming to the aid of their injured colleague.

Dugdale nodded a thank you to Turner as two shots rang out from the pathway to the side of the building as SFO Jonathan Shaw, saved by his bulletproof vest, shot dead the murderer of twenty-five-year-old PC Stephen Kitchen, whose life ebbed away at the bottom of the rear steps before a medical team could reach him.

Having ensured all other rooms were clear, the officers broke off the padlocks on the four first floor rooms to find a collection of terrified young girls, mostly in their early teens, huddled together in the far corners of rooms which all smelled of cheap perfume and urine, some wearing only G-strings and tee-shirts whilst others were naked and trying to cover themselves with grubby, unwashed duvets.

"Police, you're safe now" called out the officers who entered the sordid rooms, holding out their hands, palms facing, to reassure the occupants that they were in no danger before WPCs were called to organise the transport of the hurriedly dressed girls to a variety of Police Stations throughout Sheffield to give statements.

The killer of PC Kitchen, who had been tasked with securing the rear exit, was identified as Sean McGoldrick, a twenty-three-year-old thug from Sheffield who was well known to the Police and had previous convictions for possession of cannabis but the arrests for GBH and ABH always failed to progress through lack of witnesses, they either refused to testify or disappeared.

Following the accepted procedures, all McGoldrick's clothes were bagged and sent to Forensics, including a significant blood stain on the lower right-hand sleeve of a creased, dark, woollen overcoat.

The other Veronica's in Leeds, Bradford, York, Manchester, Newcastle, Liverpool and Hull and the Hedonism sites, were the subject of similar co-ordinated raids though fortunately with no Police casualties.

Dan and his team were responsible for interviewing the nine girls liberated from the York premises and the stories were very like the other sex-slaves.

The older girls liberated from the Sheffield premises told of three girls who had disappeared having threatened or made plans to escape, including Chloe, as they all knew her fate from copies of the Sheffield Star and accused McGoldrick as the murderer. He was the one to be feared. He was the one who beat the girls if they stepped out of line and they told their interviewers that he enjoyed inflicting pain on them, whether he had a reason or not.

The interviews took several days and it was almost a week before all the interviews were typed up and signed and the girls were given time to rest in safety, something that they never thought would come.

The bloodstains on McGoldrick's coat were matched to Chloe and were he not dead would have charged with her murder as well as PC Kitchen.

In the extensive search of the premises by the CSI teams, however, the only weapons recovered were the two used by the dead doormen, and after the ballistics report was received, they confirmed neither of these matched the bullet that killed Popescu.

So, who killed him and where was the gun?

They did not have to wait long to find out as the ballistics report from the shooting in Dover confirmed that Popescu was shot by the gun taken from Bălan. As he was now dead, it seemed to be a tidy end to the episode.

Including the girls in Sheffield, a total of one hundred and seven girls and seven boys, all young, Eastern European or Asian kidnapped sex-slaves were freed to give their damning statements in the security of Police Stations across the region.

Whilst this was happening in England and the freed slaves were being interviewed and assessed by experienced medical and psychological teams, police forces across Europe were carrying out similar raids based on information obtained from the book given to Josef Weissman by Pavel Popescu.

In Rome, a major gun battle ensued which ended with ten people dead, two police officers, six Rumanians and two innocent bystanders who were caught in the crossfire outside a bakery on the Via Portuense which housed a high-class brothel in the rooms above.

With the information gleaned from Popescu's ledger, the courts in all European countries froze the Rumanian Mafia's accounts, their off-shore accounts in the Cayman Islands and Mauritius and their considerable assets worldwide, effectively closing a large slice of operations.

Popescu, however, did not know all the accounts or operations as they chose to operate as individual cells, only the hierarchy knew the full scope of their business interests, to protect themselves from just such a breach of their security.

This was nevertheless a major victory for law enforcement and their task had been helped incalculably by Popescu and by Patrick in exposing and helping bring to justice the late Stefan Bălan and the captured Stuart Mullins who it was believed had been responsible for up to thirty young, vulnerable, kidnapped slaves being smuggled into the UK.

Chapter 25

Dan and his team at Northallerton were tasked with finding the murderer of Michael Adams and his second in command, Detective Sergeant James James, his parents must have had a bizarre sense of humour, had made little progress whilst Dan had been away in Dover working alongside the Kent Force.
In fact, Dan returned to more questions than answers.

If Sean McGoldrick killed Chloe, and the evidence now confirmed that he did, then who killed Michael Adams?
Not McGoldrick, that much was certain, as firstly he never left Veronica's and secondly the style of the killing. His style was extreme violence and a simple blow to the head with no follow-up butchery of the victim was not his trademark.

So, who else had a motive?

The "Family", certainly, if he had wanted a larger slice of the cake and had been naive enough to make threats and now they were aware of his need for money to satisfy his wife's lifestyle ambitions, his mortgage payments on the stables and the rising costs of running his yard, he could well have been desperate enough.
If he had been so stupid then this was a likely outcome, although a bullet to the head was more their modus operandi.

Was it a lover's tiff? Stella was known to have an explosive temper, but surely this was extreme. However, it could answer the question of why she had fled but was it because she had killed Adams? Or to escape retribution from the Rumanians for the failed operation in France?

James believed that she was involved in the trafficking even though she had covered her tracks so well that they would have great difficulty in proving that she knew anything about this side of the business. If she was ever found she would undoubtedly claim that she simply did the accounts and as far as she knew the monies were just from the transport business and her husband's betting and as a partner in the business she could take the proceeds whenever she wanted, it wasn't a crime.

Had Mullins found out about Adams' affair with his wife, he swore not when questioned by the Kent Police, but then he swore he knew nothing about the girls in the secret compartment, and only fled as he thought he was being chased by a gang of armed thieves and Bălan had told him to run.

Until that is, he and his solicitor were shown the video of the girls being loaded into the cab in France.

Could it have been Bălan, who had also been the recipient of Stella's considerable sexual favours? Possibly, but with him dead, they would not get any sensible answers from him, but again a shot to the head was his preferred style.

North Yorkshire Police also interviewed at length Alexandra Adams.

They found that the mortgages and secured loans on Monk's Lane Stables were all covered by Michael's life insurance policies, around seven hundred and fifty thousand pounds in total and with the premises debt free and with no monthly commitments, the business would not only make a substantial profit but Alexandra would be sitting on over a million pounds worth of assets including the goodwill of the business, more than enough motive for a greedy wife who almost certainly would know about his infidelity even if he was unaware of hers.

But she had an alibi that they were unable to break.

She had spent the weekend in London with a banker boyfriend and the night that Adams' had been murdered, they were having dinner together at the Savoy Grill as the Head Waiter Gervais and his staff would confirm.

The search of Mullins premises revealed little. No Mobile. No Cash. No Records. No Weapons.

Just a business account that had been cleared out with the money being transferred to a Stella Dooley, which they soon found was Stella Mullins maiden name. They quickly obtained a court order to freeze the funds in this account only to find that the account was empty, the funds being transferred to an account in Grand Cayman and after that, they lost track of the money.

After a police check of all flights, Eurostar passenger lists, and ferry crossings, there was no record of a Stella Mullins ever leaving the country. She was either in hiding or had vanished and their money was on the latter.

Searching Bălan's flat, they did find ammunition for a Glock, matching the gun they secured in Kent, but nothing else useful.

After a week of investigation, they were no nearer to finding Stella or any money but had concluded that Bălan had executed Popescu so that at least closed the book on another murder for the Yorkshire forces.

But as for who killed Michael Adams, Stella Mullins was the only one with the means, the motive, and the opportunity. The garage was full of possible murder weapons such as torque wrenches. If he had threatened to tell Mullins about the affair and jeopardised the income from the smuggling operations, that was certainly a motive and as for opportunity, no one knew where she was on the night in question and they could find no one who could give her an alibi, even Mullins, when told of her disappearance with all the cash, had refused to comment.

The Police, therefore, issued an International Arrest Warrant for Stella Mullins for the murder of Michael Adams and with the strength of Interpol and other worldwide agencies, they were confident that it was only a matter of time before she was brought to justice.

Chapter 26

Returning from Dover on Monday afternoon, Patrick found Melanie waiting for him at Oaktree Farm and entered to the aroma of freshly brewed coffee and the welcome sight of Mrs. Weston's delicious Cherry Madeira Cake.

"What are you doing here?" he enquired, "I've left half a dozen messages this morning for you as you missed your morning show".

"Dan called last night to let me know that you were safe as if I knew all about it".

"Ahh, well I didn't want to tell you before as I knew you'd worry, so what did he tell you?"

"Only that you'd been involved in a shoot-out and arrested members of the Rumanian Mafia. He wouldn't tell me anything else other than not to worry and that he was sure that you would tell me everything when you got home today. He obviously felt embarrassed that you had kept me in the dark!"

"I'm sorry but I was only thinking of you but cut me a slice of cake and I'll tell you everything over a cup of coffee".

Sitting upright in a decidedly frosty mood, a strangely quiet Melanie sat opposite Patrick across the oak kitchen table where he relayed all the details starting with the mysterious Land Rover when he moved in, the reason for Michael Adams' murder and the results of his trips to Ireland and France including the shootings and the number of girls that had been freed from their horrendous half-lives as sex-slaves.

Sounds like the script for a film, she thought, as she listened intently in almost wide-eyed disbelief, in fact, were it not Patrick telling her and knowing that he wouldn't dare to either embellish the facts or leave any out as he was aware of the trouble he was in with her, she would have thought it a fairy story.

She wasn't going to let him know how proud she was of him just yet though as she was still smouldering from being kept in the dark and he had to realise that she wouldn't put up with this if they were to become anything more than they already were.

By the time they had drunk three coffees and Patrick had demolished half of the Madeira Cake. it was dark outside and the room was lit only by the flicker of the wood-burning stove.
Melanie got up from the table and switched on the Christmas Tree lights, giving the room a warm glow and truly seasonal atmosphere, even if the atmosphere wasn't totally reflected in the relationship as Melanie spoke little and gave him the silent treatment.

Patrick knew that he should have told her. That had been made crystal clear and he tried to recall the last time that they had had a disagreement or row, and couldn't remember, it never happened, but now it had he knew how much he didn't want to risk losing her and would do all he could to make it up to her, he just hoped it wasn't too late as he genuinely had kept it close to his chest to avoid her worrying.

"Fancy going to the pub?" he enquired after a lengthy spell of the two of them just staring into the flickering fire in silence.

"Am I included", came the sarcastic retort.

"You know you are, and I am sorry, really, I did only want to protect you".

Maybe he had suffered enough? She hoped that she had made her point.

"Better get ready then as we can't stay in here all holiday".

"What do you mean all holiday", he quizzed.

"I'm here until the New Year if you want me to stay?"

"Of course I want you to stay, in fact, I don't want you to ever go back, I love you so much", he was ecstatic and knew they'd reached a major point in their relationship and he hoped that she felt the same.

"Jag älskar dig också, idiot" (I love you too) looking into his eyes, she threw her arms around his neck and kissed him long and passionately,

"Now go and get showered if we're going out".

It took a very relieved Patrick just twenty minutes to shave and shower before putting on clean jeans and a purple and white striped Ralph Lauren shirt with an emerald green motif.

He had heard Melanie in the bedroom and when he went down into the lounge she had changed into his favourite skin-tight black needle-cords and wore a denim shirt with a stand-up collar, smelling deliciously of Estee Lauder Beautiful, how much it suited her.

Wrapping up in their Barbour's and woollen scarves they walked hand-in-hand to The Margrave in the cold early evening air seeing only the ghostly white shape on a Barn Owl as it flew directly across the road in front of them to look for any sign of mice or voles for dinner.

Reaching the village and with Christmas Eve just a day away, it looked amazing, with the windows of the Village Store and Post Office and the private houses twinkling with all different styles and colours of Christmas lights, it felt just such a wonderful place and it felt like home, it only lacked snow.

As they entered the pub, they were surprised how busy it was, almost like a quiz night, until they looked down to the far end and saw five members of the Salvation Army Band setting up.
"Usual?" asked Angela, bedecked with flashing Santa Claus earrings and mistletoe adorning the front of a green and red Elf-hat trimmed with white fur.

"Yes please Angela, busy tonight." Patrick automatically replied.
"I'll just have a coke please Angela it looks like a long night, what time do they start", enquired a flushed Melanie.
"Eight o'clock and it's always a good night, Carol Sheets are on the tables. Mum's been baking mince pies all day so they'll be coming around later. Hope you're hungry she's made hundreds!"

Patrick thought they would be able to have a quiet conversation tonight but there was little chance of that as they looked around for a seat and spotted John and Charlie in their usual corner.

"Melanie", shouted Charlie and waved frantically for them to join her and John.

"Have you heard about Stuart Mullins?" an excited Charlie asked before they even sat down, "rumour is he killed Michael and his drivers have been caught smuggling, they're all locked up"

Before he could answer, Patrick's phone rang and he walked away from the group to answer.

"Hi, it's Dan, where are you?"

"In the pub"

"Is Melanie with you?" he asked with a note of concern.

"Yes mate".

"I'm sorry Patrick, I never dreamed that she wouldn't know. Is everything OK?"

"Yes, we're fine thanks and it's my fault, not yours".

"OK, see you", and simply hung up.

Patrick wondered why Dan had hung up but assumed he had been interrupted.

By the time he returned to the table the girls were talking about Christmas so he chose to speak to John about racing over Christmas and the New Year.

As soon as Charlie found that Melanie was staying at Oaktree for Christmas she immediately invited them over for supper one night and said they would try to find a night as she didn't know yet when they were visiting her family and this had to be a priority as they were meeting Patrick for the first time.

Charlie saw that Melanie was drinking coke and decided to join her when John asked what they would like, "I remember the last time I drank with her", she joked, "I don't want to repeat that, I lived off paracetamol for the next 36 hours".

The pub filled even more as it seemed the Sally Army Band was an annual occasion and most of the village came along to sing carols and eat Lindsay Castle's fabulous mince pies as an official start to their Christmases.

Just as the band started, Patrick saw Dan at the bar talking to Peter Castle and thought he caught a glimpse of Nayna, although she was so small she was would be lost in the crowd if she was with him.

Dan saw Patrick and put up his hand before easing his way through the crowd followed by Nayna almost holding onto the tail of Dan's jacket as she didn't know how she would get through the crowd on her own.

"Evening all," Dan said jokingly before Patrick introduced Dan and Nayna to John and Charlie.

John stood and gave his seat to Nayna as there was no chance of finding any more seats tonight.

Seeing that they didn't have a glass, Patrick was about to ask them what they wanted as a stressed and perspiring, red-faced Peter Castle pushed his way through to the table and set down an ice bucket with a bottle of Moet and Chandon and six gleaming champagne glasses.

"What are we celebrating?" Charlie piped up.

"Patrick's success with the operation and the other news that we have arrested twenty-six members of the Rumanian Mafia across Europe and freed over two hundred and fifty girls who were abducted and forced to work as sex-slaves, so this my friend is on me and I have to tell you that you deserve "a medal as big as a dustbin lid" according to the Chief Constable, so cheers mate, well done", as he poured six glasses of the chilled bubbly in almost perfectly even measures.

"Sorry Melanie, everything OK?" Dan asked almost as an afterthought as she may have been OK with Patrick but he suddenly realised that he may be in the doghouse for spilling the beans.
"Perfect, thank you, Dan".
"Good".

Melanie thought that Charlie's chin was about to bounce off her knees.
"You didn't say anything earlier when I asked", she exclaimed looking straight at Melanie.
"I thought I'd let Patrick tell you when he had chance, but with this noise", as right on cue, the band started their repertoire with "Hark the Herald Angels Sing" making any further conversation impossible until the break, when Lindsay's warm mince pies were delivered ten to a plate to each table and large serving plates piled high at various places along the bar.
The hungry customers made short work of them and Lindsay busily refilled the plates to choruses of thanks, no one was sure whether her glowing red cheeks were because of the warmth of the pub or the warmth of the compliments.

With such a crowded pub, Dan's revelations had been heard by all the surrounding people and the story had spread through the pub like wildfire during the interval and Patrick was the centre of attention with people wondering just how they could ask the question as their curiosity was killing them.

The band must have had almost second sight as they kicked off the second half with "Good King Wenceslas" before anyone plucked up the courage to ask and with the drinks and the satisfying food, the throng began to sing along using the song sheets that had been lying largely unused on the tables during the first half. The singing was helped tremendously by the elder members of the church choir who had forced their way into the pub after choir practice which started at seven-thirty and were obviously keen to sample the mince pies.

Charlie in typical fashion had forgotten she was only drinking soft drinks tonight and had finished her champagne before anyone else and amid the singing looked sideways at Melanie as she swapped Melanie's full, untouched glass with her empty one and Melanie picked up her half-drunk glass of coke without anyone noticing.

The evening epitomised Christmas, with the brass band, carol singing, mince pies and champagne all under the enchantment of The Margrave's beautifully decorated Christmas tree.

The bar staff had made a great deal of effort to dress for the occasion with tinsel, bells and novelty earrings embellishing their green, red and white Christmas Elf costumes and absorbed in this typical village Christmas, Melanie felt completely at home.

As everyone dug deep into their pockets and wallets to generously fill the white, plastic bucket that the band passed around before the final carol, "O Come All Ye Faithful" brought their evening to an end, Dan and Nayna made their excuses to leave as they only had babysitters until eleven o'clock as this was all last minute, they promised however to meet over the holiday.

"I'll call you tomorrow and fill you in on everything," Dan said making a phone gesture with his little finger and thumb.

How busy were they going to be, they would struggle to fit everything in Melanie thought?

They left the pub to a chorus of "Goodnights and Merry Christmases", as by now pretty much everyone had some idea of Patrick's heroics and he wondered just how swollen his reputation had become given that he knew how much stories grew when passing from one person to another.

Walking home with John and Charlie, still sober tonight, Patrick explained what had happened with Mullins after the tip off from Justin and his escapades in France and Dover.

He was still unaware just what could have happened to make Dan turn up with the champagne, how so many villains could have been arrested and how the Police could have rescued so many girls.

At least Dan would let him know tomorrow and it had been a long few days.

"Coming in for a coffee?" Patrick asked as they approached an Oaktree Farm with the outside Christmas lights giving a wonderful festive feel but before John could accept, Charlie tugged at his arm and answered for both,
"Not tonight thanks, Patrick, I'm a bit too tired" whilst looking straight at Melanie.

As they walked on, leaving Patrick and Melanie to walk up the gravelled driveway, John questioned,
"Are you really too tired? I thought you would have jumped at the chance of a nightcap, I hope they're not offended".
"No I'm fine, we'll have a brandy at home, I was just thinking of Melanie".
"Oh, alright", John was still completely unaware.

Melanie awoke on Christmas Eve to the sounds of Chris Evans on Radio 2 downstairs. She could hear Mrs. Weston singing quietly in the kitchen and looked across at the silently breathing Patrick, "What time must it be?" she thought to herself before getting up to look over Patrick at the alarm clock. "Goodness, quarter past nine". She kissed Patrick who woke immediately,
"Come on sleepyhead, we've got a very busy day"

"Why, what do we have to do?"

"Well, have you made any plans for tomorrow, you know, Christmas Day?"

"Oh shit, no".

"Language young man", it was unusual for Patrick to swear in front of Melanie which she thought was novel and very gentlemanly.

"We haven't made any plans, though; we haven't even spoken about what are we doing for Christmas Dinner".

"All taken care of", he pronounced showing off.

"What do you mean?"

"We've been invited to John and Charlie's if that's OK?"

"Yes, perfect, but we'll need to take some wine and chocolates and things".

"I know; we'll go shopping but it'll be like a football match everywhere today".

"Well I have something to do this morning so if you give me a list I'll get it and you can tell me over breakfast how long we've got together this holiday and all the things you want to do".

Patrick showered first.

He actually wanted to shower together but somehow wasn't comfortable with Mrs. Weston downstairs knowing that Melanie could get quite noisy, so putting on an old pair of jeans and a worn bright red Hilfiger sweatshirt, he went downstairs where the aroma of his freshly brewed coffee was a perfect way to greet the day.

"Morning Mrs. Weston, bright and early this morning?"

"Good morning, yes, lots to do today. I've got to go to Tesco and the Farm Shop after I finish here, we're having all the family tomorrow for Christmas Dinner so lots to do, mince pies to bake, ham to roast, lots of things".

"Well stop what you're doing and go home. Melanie's here over Christmas and I'm sure we can look after ourselves for a few days".

"Are you sure? I'm happy to work through?"

"I'm sure you are, here's your wages and a Christmas Bonus," he said producing an extra £250 from his wallet which he retrieved from his jacket which he had thrown onto the sofa last night "That should buy your turkey at least".

"Oh Mr. Spencer, are you sure?"

"Of course now get off home and look after the family and don't come back until the New Year, look at it as holiday pay!" he grinned.

"Thank you", she said grabbing her coat from the back of a dining chair, "Merry Christmas to you both".

"Merry Christmas to you too", as the sound of Melanie heaving into the bathroom toilet made its way downstairs.

"So that's why she drank coke," he thought to himself, "She's got an upset stomach"

She came downstairs desperate for a glass of fresh orange juice and drank two full glasses as the colour slowly returned to her cheeks.

"Feeling better?"

"Yes thanks, must have been something I ate".

"Breakfast?"

"Just dry toast please", as she retired to the sofa leaving Patrick to fix her breakfast as she started to write him a shopping list.

"So when do you have to go back?" he asked, dreading the answer.

"Can we talk about that later; I think I'm going back to bed for an hour".

"Of course, do you want me to pick up any Alka-Seltzers or anything for your tummy?" he was pleased to put it off, "let's worry about you going back after Christmas", he said, rapidly pushing it to the back of his mind.

After breakfast, leaving Melanie to rest, he left to drive into Leeds before calling at the Tesco store on Clifton Moor and the Black Bull Farm Shop to tick off all the items on Melanie's long shopping list and like most men shoppers, a good few extra items that took his fancy, luxuries not necessities, but it was only Christmas once a year he told himself justifying the expense.

By the time he returned home Melanie looked fully recovered and was on the phone to Melissa who had been reading the morning papers, in particular the article about the shooting in Dover and the mention of "Writer Patrick Spencer who apprehended the ringleader". She said she would tell her all about it on Boxing Day and she was looking forward to seeing her sister and the rest of the family, it was a long time since they had been together at Christmas.

Patrick firstly proceeded to unload the car and secondly tried hard to find space in the fridge for the ham, beef and turkey he had bought, along with pork pies, vol-au-vents, sausage rolls, bacon, sausages and enough other food to see them through to February should six feet of snow suddenly descend and they be cut off from the outside world for a month.

"Melissa says that you are a hero in the morning papers, she read the article to me. She's very impressed and looking forward to meeting you on Boxing Day."
"We're going to see the family on Boxing Day, are we?"
"Too late to back out now".
"It's OK, I'll start psyching myself up for it".
"Oh and we're staying over as well, that's OK, isn't it?"
"Whatever you want darling". He was still making up, even if it wasn't necessary, just as Dan rang.

He told him all about the call from Weissman and the identification of the body of Novotny as Popescu. Interpol had organised a co-ordinated swoop on premises across Europe and the information in Popescu's ledger had enabled the authorities to confiscate over £360m of assets belonging to the Rumanian Mafia with enough evidence to ensure convictions of all the members arrested and the future arrests of a large number who were now on wanted lists worldwide.

The girls and young boys who had been abducted would never be the same again, that much was obvious, but they would now lead lives as normal as they could make them and the operation had saved many hundreds or potentially thousands of others from the same fate.

This was still on his mind and he didn't feel like another night out, even though she seemed to be fine now when he asked.

"What do you want to do tonight?"

"Can we just stay in by the fire? I'll light some candles and we'll see if you have bought anything to eat?"

"Bought something to eat", he replied in mock outrage, "I have just about emptied the chiller cabinets at the Black Bull just so that I could spoil you this holiday, honung (honey)".

"Feel free to spoil me whenever you wish and who's been learning Swedish then clever clogs?"

"Nothing is beyond me you know", he chuckled, pleased he had pronounced it correctly.

After a very relaxing day watching old films on TV, dozing in front of the log fire, they were mesmerised by the red, yellow and gold flames, they eventually decided about eight o'clock to have a light supper of Stilton and Crackers, completely ignoring the obscene about of food that was crammed into the fridge and weighing down the shelves of the kitchen cupboards, before shuffling, yawning up to bed at ten o'clock.

Chapter 27

Christmas morning.

They both awoke at seven o'clock. It was still dark outside but as Patrick looked out he could see the trees and fields covered in a heavy, hoar frost, not snow but picturesque nevertheless.

"Merry Christmas", he beamed as he kissed Melanie and thought of the day ahead and just how lucky he was to have found her.
"God Jul till dig också" (Merry Christmas to you too) she replied as she jumped out of bed and ran to the En-suite toilet where she threw up.
"Oh no, not Christmas morning," he thought to himself.
"Are you OK?", he called when the retching had stopped.
"I'm fine. Will you get breakfast for us, I'll be down in few minutes?"
"OK. What do you fancy?"
"Just toast and orange juice please".

Patrick took the opportunity to carry downstairs a paper sack full of carefully wrapped presents for Melanie that he had been hiding in the study and hid them behind her sofa.
After he had put some logs on the burner with some firelighters for ease and speed, as the fire had gone out overnight, he put the beans in the coffee maker and put a couple of slices of wholemeal bread into the toaster. It didn't taste the same as toast on the open fire but needs must.

Melanie appeared right on time, wrapped in his heavy brown dressing gown, just as he was pouring his first coffee.

"Coffee?"

"No just orange juice please, I hope you bought plenty of it?"

"Gallons!"

"Just a glass will be fine to start with", she laughed.

"You need to take something for that stomach, I picked up some Alka-Seltzer yesterday if you want a couple?"

"No thanks I'm fine with orange juice and toast," she said looking at the clock and walking to stare out of the kitchen window.

"Looking for snow?"

"No, I just wondered what the weather was like".

Having given Melanie her toast, he began to warm his croissants in the microwave, even Christmas morning began with croissants, when she put her plate down and walked to the kitchen door as Patrick heard a vehicle on the gravelled drive.

"Who can that be, don't they know it's Christmas morning?" he grumbled.

"It's alright, it's for me", she replied mysteriously.

"Stay in the house", and with that she closed the door behind her.

A few minutes later she came in and handed him a blanket containing a tiny bundle of black fur that looked up at him with pleading eyes,

"Merry Christmas Älskling, he's 9 weeks old and his name's Oscar", as an uncharacteristically emotional and speechless Patrick held his beautiful new pet Labrador puppy.

It took a good two minutes before he looked into Melanie's eyes and could only say "Thank you".

He handed Oscar back to Melanie and walked behind the sofa to her present sack and fetched out a present which was beautifully wrapped in a different wrapping paper to her other presents.
Keeping his hands behind his back he handed the small square package to her while taking hold of Oscar.
She tried to think of anything else that could be in a box this small as she carefully unwrapped the present.

As she opened the box Patrick, putting Oscar down to explore the kitchen, took the two-carat diamond solitaire ring from the box and on one knee took her hand and inquired with trepidation "vill du gifta dig med mig Melanie Karlsson?"
Melanie cried.
"Yes, of course, I will marry you" and Patrick slipped the ring onto her finger and looking into each other's watery eyes, kissed in front of the fire.
They turned to find Oscar sitting and looking up at them with his head cocked to one side when they both burst into fits of laughter, scaring the puppy who went to hide behind the sofa.
"Thank you for agreeing to be my wife and for the best Christmas present ever", trembled a grateful and ecstatic Patrick.
"You're welcome, and anyway every child should have a dog to grow up with".
"You're right" Patrick paused, his mind in a whirl as he thought he understood what she was saying.

"You don't mean? How? Well, I mean I know how but why? I mean when? I don't actually know what I mean!"

"You're going to be a daddy in the summer, July to be precise".

"I can't believe it, who knows?"

"Only us, but I'm sure that Charlie has guessed so we can tell them at lunchtime".

"So that's why you're sick and only drinking pop and juice?"

"Yes. I thought we'd tell the family together tomorrow. But I only thought we'd be telling them that we're having a baby, not that we're getting married."

"We'll have to take Oscar with us, will that be OK?"

"Of course it will, they'll love him. And you". she laughed.

"What will we do about food and all the other stuff, it's Christmas Day, nowhere is open?"

"It's all outside in a big box together with his new bed. Bring it in, will you? I'll see if he wants a drink".

The morning passed in a daze and it was only an hour later that Patrick realised that he had not given Melanie the rest of her presents which she opened excitedly, but with a sense of anti-climax.

He wondered excitedly how Pam would take to the news that she was going to be an auntie, perhaps it would bring them a little closer together?

One of the good things about having a pregnant fiancée is that she can drive whilst you can have a drink so they decided to drive the mile or so to Margrave Stables armed with bottles of champagne, (that's why she had put them on the shopping list!) Barolo Italian red wine, and a nice bottle of Hennessey Bras D'Or Cognac.

Wrapping Oscar in his red woollen blanket and taking his food and water dishes, they set off for lunch at two o'clock and were greeted with a glass of champagne and ushered into the huge dining kitchen where the lads that had not gone home for Christmas were gathered for Christmas Lunch along with young stable jockey Cath Sullivan, who was also Charlie's cousin and blessed with the same red hair and freckles as Charlie.

Everyone rushed to make a fuss of the adorable little puppy who appeared to welcome all the attention but disgraced himself by peeing all over Head Lad Simon Johnson.

Melanie, however, made straight for Charlie who had her back turned and was checking the veg on the AGA. She tapped Charlie on her shoulder and she turned to see Melanie flashing her engagement ring, as she announced to the guests "I hope we're not hijacking your party but we have an announcement to make, Patrick has asked me to marry him and I've said yes."
Everyone clapped and whooped at the beaming couple before Charlie teased,

"Is that everything or do you have something else to tell us, Melanie?"
"Yes alright, I'm pregnant"
A chorus of fantastic and congratulations rang out as everyone wanted to shake hands and John opened two bottles of Moet and Chandon before asking the guests to raise their glasses to the future mum and dad.
The ensuing round of applause was followed by Charlie asking "So you'll be moving into Oaktree Farm for good then Melanie?"

Melanie could see by his expression that the thought had not yet occurred to Patrick, but putting him out of his misery,

"Yes, of course", she giggled, looking into Patrick's eyes, she watched the reality of her acceptance begin to sink in.

Over Charlie's champagne and Melanie's orange juice, Charlie excitedly confided in her,
"It'll be great having you here all the time, I've never really had a best friend since I left school and there'll be so much to do together with you and the baby, it's brilliant".
Melanie had to admit that the two of them hit it off from that first night and it would be good for her too and with Nayna only a few miles away and Patrick being close to John and Dan it did feel like home already.

Charlie was a great cook and was obviously used to cooking for big parties as Christmas Dinner proved.

As well as cooking for nine people she still found plenty of time to talk to everyone and play the perfect host, just as John did pouring generous measures of any drink that took their fancy for his lads, telling jokes and letting everyone see the real John, not merely an employer.

Christmas Dinner at three o'clock was huge and served on large oval plates that Charlie kept specifically for Christmas Dinner and for a cold meats and pickles day with homemade chips on Boxing Day.

Homemade Chicken Liver and Brandy pate and Melba Toast, just the Toast and Orange Juice again for Melanie, was followed by a huge plate of Roast Turkey with all the trimmings and a heavy, sumptuously alcoholic Christmas Pudding. The cheese board to end the meal was fit to grace any restaurant in the country with no less than six different English cheeses and an array of fruits. She was so sure that Melanie was pregnant that she had made her a French Apple Tart and Custard, just in case!

By the end of the meal Patrick thought he would do well to make it to the car, but he had thoughtfully been very restrained with the Wine, Port and Brandy as he didn't want to fall asleep when they got home, not wanting to miss a single minute of this amazing day and he had to drive to London tomorrow to meet his future in-laws, so needed to be on his best behaviour or his Fiancée would kill him!

He held Oscar wrapped in his blanket in the passenger seat and marvelled at the prospects of what the future held.

He ended Christmas Day with a Fiancée instead of a girlfriend, a fantastic little puppy that he had wanted a long time and in July he would be a father.

As days went, they just couldn't get any better than this, could they?

Chapter 28

As Patrick loaded the car on Boxing Day morning, he thought to himself that packing Oscar's bed, food, dishes, lead, and blanket was somehow preparing him for when the baby came, it was just as well that they had the Range Rover.

Melanie was still throwing up in the bathroom as he put their case in the boot and he hoped that she would be alright to travel?

Walking back inside, Oscar had found his way around the house and was happily chasing a rubber ball that Melanie had bought him until it went scooting under the sofa where he couldn't reach it and having given up trying to retrieve it, he sat hidden by the coffee table and tried his first attempt at a bark which Patrick roared with laughter at.

A pale but showered Melanie made her way downstairs to the by now customary wholemeal toast and orange juice breakfast that Patrick had prepared for her.

Three-quarters of an hour later they set off for London to meet the parents with Oscar asleep on Melanie's knee in the rear seat, curled up in his red blanket.

Patrick was not nervous at meeting her parents but wanted to make a good impression for her sake as they were now going to be family.

He still couldn't believe that they were going to be married and be parents, this would be the first of a lifetime of get-togethers so starting on the right foot was very important.

He had only reached Malton when he whispered to Melanie,

"We'll have to start to choose some names?"

"Steady on älskling, we've not even had the first scan yet so we have no idea whether it's a boy or a girl".

"Definitely a girl".

"Sure, are we?"

"Absolutely".

"How come?"

"Just a feeling, and she'll be just like you, tiny and sick!"

"Just because I'm pregnant doesn't mean I can't give you a thump".

He could hardly contain his excitement with everything that had happened and lulled into a thoughtful calm for a few miles until Melanie broke the silence,

"I wonder what mum and dad will say, it will be their first grandchild?"

"I'm more concerned about what they will think of your choice of husband?"

"They'll love you, you are just dad's type of man".

"He likes James Bond, then does he?"

"Big Head! No, but seriously I know he works in the City but he hardly has a good word to say about the bankers and traders he deals with, so I know he'll be impressed with you. I do wonder though what Melissa's new man is like?"

"Why the concern?"

"Well based on her past record he could be a Mafia hitman!"

Patrick laughed, "I'm sure that's a bit over the top, when I've heard you two on the phone she sounds just like you".

"On the phone maybe, but just wait and see and don't say I didn't warn you".

They reached the A1M and headed south towards the M18 and M1 to the M25 and on to Ascot where Klaus and Annelise, his future in-laws lived.

The traffic was very light with scarcely a truck or coach in sight and the journey which Patrick expected to take five hours took just less than four, pulling into the driveway of the most impressive ten-year-old new build red brick detached property which must be worth all of £5,000,000.

For the first time since meeting Melanie, he realised just how wealthy her family was.

It had never occurred to him before but it was now a further concern that her father, in view of the family fortune, may feel the need to vet him as a suitor.

He felt a bit less confident of himself but nevertheless could not care less whether Melanie was wealthy or a pauper, he loved her and she was having his child, nothing else mattered.

When they pulled up Melissa ran screaming towards the car and threw her arms around Melanie scarcely able to contain her excitement, goodness knows how she will cope with the news we have for them, he thought to himself.

Klaus and Annelise walked to greet them and Melanie introduced them with handshakes and smiles all around.

Only Melissa's new man, Guy, waited at the door to greet them with what Patrick regarded as a cautious welcome. Maybe he was just nervous at meeting the famous sister. Patrick opened the back door and picked up Oscar and proudly held him to face his new family.
"Melanie said it would be alright if we brought our new addition", beamed a proud Patrick and the women cooed and fell for the little bundle straight away, almost fighting to hold him as Patrick gathered their overnight bags and Oscar's many accompaniments.

Walking through the light-oak front door which shone as if treated with yacht varnish, Guy held out his hand,
"Nice to meet you both, I've heard a lot about you", pressing Patrick's hand strongly and looking him daringly in the eye.
"You too, Guy".

"Ready for a beer?" Klaus asked the two boys leading them into the massive designer kitchen which could have come straight from Home and Garden magazine.
"Why not?" was the unanimous reply as screams echoed from the lounge.
"Klaus, come here quickly" shouted a thrilled Annelise, Patrick noticed immediately the strong Swedish accent which was such a contrast to Melanie.

Klaus rolled his eyes as he walked through into the lounge followed by the others carrying their opened, ice-cold, Pistonhead Kustom Premium Swedish Lager, maybe Klaus was a connoisseur?

Klaus showed little emotion, unlike the rest of the family, as Melanie showed off her engagement ring, simply saying "Congratulations" and smiling at Patrick as he walked back into the kitchen.

A loud "pop!" was heard followed by a ringing of fine crystal glasses as they were brought down from the diamond patterned, leaded glass fronted kitchen cabinet.
Klaus carried the tray of glasses as well as the chilled Bollinger and laid them on the antique Chinese dresser and began to pour.
Melanie beckoned Patrick to come over to her, Melissa was still fussing Oscar.

"Not for me Dad thanks, we have some other news. You are going to be grandparents in July"

Annelise cried.

Followed by Melissa and it looked as though Klaus would not be far behind them as Oscar peed over Melissa.

"You'll have a glass Patrick?" radiated Klaus.

"Of course".

"Cheers everyone", after Klaus had handed everyone a glass of the chilled bubbly, "Here's to our wonderful family and the family yet to come".

"Do you think they were pleased with the news?" Patrick asked when they were unpacking upstairs in a massive En-suite guest room.

"Pleased, I think that is the understatement of the year. I thought Mum was never going to stop crying and I've never seen Dad like that before, he's never been known to show his feelings, even to us. Pity Oscar peed on Melissa though", she laughed.

"What do you think of Guy?" she questioned.

"Well maybe it's just the occasion but I feel like I know him from somewhere, but I can't remember where. Maybe it will come to me"

They went down after showering to the aroma of garlic and spices and jovial voices coming from the Kitchen.

Carrying Oscar to ensure that he didn't spoil the extensive expanse of cream carpet, they were greeted enthusiastically by a family who had a lot to take in but nevertheless were very happy to have their children under their roof once again, obviously evoking happy memories.

More champagne and beer was followed by excellent wines followed by more champagne and brandy and Patrick realised that whilst he and Guy were feeling the effects, Klaus was as sober as a judge, obviously well-practised, thought Patrick.

After a supper of Garlic Chicken or Indian Spiced Lamb, yes there was a choice! fresh fruits, chocolate fudge cake and honeycomb ice cream, everyone politely declined the offer of the cheeseboard.

Klaus asked Melanie to play the Grand Piano in the hallway and Patrick realised that although he knew that she had been trained by a maestro he had never heard her play. He soon appreciated how good she was, even to his ear, and began to think where they could fit a piano into Oaktree for Melanie to teach their daughter.

Klaus insisted on a round of brandies after which Melissa, with a slightly unsteady Guy, went up to bed, kissing everyone goodnight and feeling fortunate to belong to such a loving family, even if they didn't get together often enough.

Shortly afterwards, Annelise encouraged Melanie to say goodnight leaving Klaus with Patrick and a bottle of Cognac.

Melanie suspected that this was to be a father to future son-in-law chat and chuckled aloud leaning on her mother as they walked upstairs.

When alone, Klaus's expression changed and Patrick wondered just what was coming.

"I'm very pleased that you are going to part of the family Patrick, I know that you make my daughter very happy and with the baby, I, well we are pleased that you are making it more official but can I speak to you in confidence?"

"Of course, what is it?"

"It's about Guy. I built this business up by being able to judge people and knowing who to trust, but then checking them out anyway. I know that Melissa is besotted with him but when I checked Guy out, my people say that he doesn't exist. I want to ask if you could make some enquiries on my behalf with your contacts in the force?"

Patrick looked at Klaus trying to weigh up the man when he continued.

"One day, all of this and the business will belong to my girls, I need to be sure that they are secure so, yes, you are right, I also had you checked out", Klaus confirmed, knowing that Patrick had understood.

Patrick laughed and Klaus knew that he liked this man, his future son-in-law.

"Just me and you?" Patrick asked.

"Yes", replied Klaus.

"Ok, but there is something you should know first. I told Melanie that I thought I knew him from somewhere but couldn't place him. I lied. I am sure that his name is Adam Jarvis and we put him away for life for kidnapping a child, Sophie Brooks. Sophie died".

THE END

All characters and organisations in this book are fictional and any reference to actual organisations or persons either living or dead is entirely coincidental.

I hope that you have enjoyed this book and please visit my website at www.owenseymour.com

Printed in Great Britain
by Amazon